Tarts with Darts

by

Karen Stanley

Copyright © 2020 Karen Stanley. Published by Fabrian Books.

All rights reserved. This book or any portion thereof may not be reproduced or used in any manner without the express written permission of the publisher, except for the use of brief quotations in a book review.

Typesetting and Design Fabrian Books – fabrianbooks.com.

Karen Stanley asserts the right to be identified as the author of this book. Tarts with Darts and all the characters and events in this book are fictional. Any resemblance to individuals is purely unintentional.

About the Author

Karen Stanley is a former hairdresser, teacher and now author. Karen is also a super proud wife, mummy and even prouder Nanny! She is passionate about books and loves to write chick lit style fiction. Karen really enjoys the lighter side of life and tries to add real-life humour to her stories, collecting 'you couldn't make it up' type moments wherever she goes. Karen's books are designed to include characters that her readers can identify with, laugh with, occasionally sympathise with, and hopefully provide just the right amount of escapism.

Karen is also a budding vlogger, having dragged herself into the baffling world of technology (with a little help from her son and daughter-in-law!). She is on FB and Twitter, so why not join her there too?@KarenStanleyAuthor or @KStanleyAuthor

Karen also writes children's fiction and especially loves reading and writing poetry. She runs creative writing workshops for children in libraries, schools and bookshops and these focus on the creative process that inspires writing. You can find out more about Karen's children's work on her Facebook page @writesmarteducation

This book is dedicated to my long-suffering husband who is very often my sounding board for new ideas!

To my son and daughter-in-law for their love and support and

To my new 'family' – Fabrian Books (especially Jo Bartlett) without whose support and expertise, I would still be lost, wandering aimlessly about, in the publishing jungle!

Chapter One: Jude

Jude looked across at the sleeping form of her husband. His hands were clasped across his ample belly, his mouth slightly open as he snored gently. She sipped on her camomile tea, praying for the 'calming' effect that it so boldly promised. She glanced at the clock – 6pm – and wondered how soon she could leave the house without the inevitable 'Spanish inquisition' from Dean. Ironic really; how the only time he so much as noticed her existence was when she was either not there or preparing to be... 'not there.'

In Dean's eyes, his wife's only reason for existence lay in her ability to cook, clean and pander to his every whim – Jude was pretty sure he'd let her wipe his arse for him if she offered.

She wondered if she had ever *truly* been in love with Dean when she had entered into matrimonial bless with him almost 30 years ago. She had been 19. Wide eyed, and not so innocent, she had been the reluctant recipient of the inevitable 'bun in the oven;' as was the fate of many a naïve young thing back then. In those days, it was a lot easier to marry your bloke, than it was to leave him and spend the next 20 years raising a child alone, with no such luxury as child support – or any support for that matter.

Her mother had warned her about her choice in men, but Jude had been young and hopeful. Back then; Dean - or 'Deano' to his mates - had been a bit of a catch. A real wide boy, with a twinkle in his eye and the gift of the gab; not to mention a MkV Cortina and a gold sovereign ring. Unfortunately, the 'ducking and diving,' and 'wheeling and dealing,' that had rendered him cash rich in his youth, had led to a succession of hair-brained schemes that never came to anything much throughout his adult life.

Jude looked around at the shabby council house that they had shared for three decades. Dean was the sort of person who, 'lived for the moment' - which basically meant he squandered every penny he had as soon as he earnt it and had fuck all to show for it. He didn't *do* house improvements because the house, "didn't belong to them," and he didn't see why he should spend his money, "turning the council's place into a fucking palace!"

Jude sincerely doubted Dean's ability to turn anything into a slightly improved hovel, let alone a 'fucking palace,' as he'd never stuck to anything long enough to become any good at it. He had no trade, and certainly no taste, and he was distinctly lacking in anything that even slightly resembled a work ethic. So here they lived, in this decaying prison, complete with its chipped paintwork, worn carpets and hand-me-down furniture. Occasionally Dean would do a 'blinding' deal and come home with some revoltingly tacky artefact such as the 'Queen Anne' repro armchair in which Jude now sat, and which she very much doubted was the investment Dean thought it was. Dean's 'deals' were usually just the result of someone else off-loading their crap. More often than not, the 'investments' were worth half of fuck-all and looked distinctly out of place amongst all the other crap that they had accumulated.

In the early days, Jude had tried so hard to build a home for them, doing her best to make the place look stylish; but she had grown increasingly tired of trying to polish a giant turd for a man who was unappreciative in the extreme.

When little Dean had been born, Jude had harboured such high hopes for her young family; showering love on the boy, nurturing him, and praying that he would grow into a man of substance. Depressingly, the moment he had hit his teenage years, he had gone down the same route as many of the other boys on the estate; not helped by the fact that his feckless father had thought it a huge joke each time the boy had come home pissed or had been engaged in yet another run-in with the local constabulary.

Jude had been dead against naming little Dean after his father; she had much preferred Jake or Sam, but Dean wouldn't hear of it. It was as if naming his son after himself was an endorsement of his virility, as well as the perfect way to show the *whole* world just what a successful father he was.

Giving him his name, had been just about the sum-total of Dean's parenting input. Ironic really, for a man to profess to so much love for a boy in whom he had been so spectacularly disinterested - until such time as he was able to smoke or drink Fosters that was.

Even in the early years, Jude had felt an uneasy sense of foreboding of the possibility of 'like father, like son' – especially when your father happened to be Dean Senior.

Initially, when little Dean had begun his descent into the under belly of humanity, Jude had shed many unheard tears. She had waited by the phone for news of tragedy, or an unexpected knock at the door in the early hours. She often had no notion of where he had been for an entire night – sometimes several nights. She had begged him to get back into school, pleaded with him to find a job, offered her heart and soul to support him; but to no avail. Big Dean's only input had been to berate her for; "spoiling the boy's fun."

"Let the boy become a man," he'd said.

Jude hadn't dared answered that remark!

These days Jude had literally cried herself dry. She had given up sobbing and begging. She had given up wishing that she had taken him away when he was still her baby boy; before he was irrevocably tarnished. She hadn't been able to save him from the influences around him - she hadn't been able to save him from himself. If she'd had the courage to save herself, then maybe things might have been different. She was too tired to wish any longer – wishing got you nowhere.

Little Dean's latest escapade had meant that he was now on remand, awaiting trial for a botched burglary on some poor old lady's house. He and another 'lost' boy, had scared the poor old dear senseless when they'd broken into her home. They had demanded money but, they had very soon discovered, that she was indeed NOT hiding a secret stash of priceless jewels in her one bed council flat. The terrified woman had pleaded with them to have mercy as she had nothing to give.

What happened next beggared belief - even for Jude's low expectations of her son's intelligence. The two idiots had said that they would take a cheque – a *cheque*, for fuck's sake! And, as the old lady (who was obviously not quite as naïve as they'd expected), had innocently asked to whom she should make the cheque payable, Dean junior had given his real name; and *all* under the watchful eye of the concealed CCTV camera that the 'innocent' old dear had installed after a string of recent burglaries!

Young Dean had been recorded saying, "Now that's how you do it son; 1500 quid. Not bad for a night's work!"

Sadly, Jude was really hoping that her only son be given a long sentence. It was probably his only chance to get away from the gaggle of fuckwits who he stupidly presumed were his 'friends' and also, away from the thugs who were most likely selling him whatever shit it was that he was shovelling up his nose. Jude didn't have proof of course, but she was no fool, and she had watched her boy turn into the moody, angry, and generally dislikeable individual that he had become; with little or no concern for anyone else. He certainly had no respect for her *or* his father and, considering Dean Senior was no shining beacon of an example, what hope was there?

Jude knew that she had become totally apathetic. She had neither the energy nor the inclination to give even one shit - let alone two - and so, she drifted from day to day, cleaning a house she was ashamed of, caring for a husband whom she had no respect for, and trying to forget about the son who she couldn't save from himself.

Jude had tried to get a job several times over the years, but Dean had always put a stop to her efforts; mainly because he didn't want the DSS knocking on their door. He certainly didn't need to worry about the tax man – he hadn't been on their records his whole life!

So, for now, her only pleasures in life were; walking her dog, and ladies' Darts on a Thursday night.

Jude looked at the clock again, pushing the whole sob story of her wasted life to the back of her mind. 6.15pm. She reckoned if she snuck out the back door quietly, she could leave now. Darts didn't start till 7, but she could take a slow stroll. She'd showered and dried her hair earlier in the day, and she always kept a make-up kit in her bag for times such as this when she needed to sneak out without drawing attention to herself. If she stayed much longer, Dean would be awake and then she'd have at least half an hour of; "Where's my bloody shirt, what have you been doing all day?" or "What you getting all tarted up for?"

He'd never actually hit her, (inwardly she chastised herself for even daring to be thankful for this), but he had ground her down over the years with his constant carping. She wasn't entirely sure that her ears even worked properly anymore.

She stood up from her chair and tiptoed through to the kitchen. Her bag and coat were draped over one of the mis-matched kitchen chairs; placed for a quick getaway. As she pulled the back door shut behind her, she heard Dean shout at her from the living room.

"Jude!... JUUUUDE!"

She quickened her pace down the path toward the back gate. Once through the gate, her pounding heart slowed as she made her bid for freedom - albeit for a few hours – like a thief in the night.

Chapter Two: The Labour Club

Jude walked through the door of the social club that was home to her Ladies Darts team. She remembered the first time she had come here for a night out with Dean, on one of the rare occasions when he had invited her along, and indeed one of even fewer occasions, when she had actually agreed to come with him. Seeing as she barely tolerated his company at the best of times, a whole evening of Dean with a belly full of beer and a big gob, was not something she endured willingly.

It was tragic really; how shabby the place was but still how much cosier it felt than home. The heavily patterned red carpet was so worn in places that you could see concrete below it and, if you stood still for too long, you were highly likely to stick to it! Scratched, wooden chairs, upholstered in a myriad of mis-matching velour fabrics were scattered haphazardly around the room – some around tables, some seemingly just dumped where they had landed. The room was cavernous; a long bar stretching the entire length down one side as far as the eye could see, leading to a tired set of French doors that lead out into the 'garden.' The garden was basically a small, slabbed area next to the bins which was also home to a disused beer barrel, two broken bar stools, and an old chest freezer which served as a resting place for the backsides of dedicated smokers who would venture out in all weathers for a crafty fag.

The area to the right of the entrance door boasted a dance floor of about 6 square foot, upon which punters were encouraged to strut their funky stuff on a Saturday night when the resident band, (with an average age of about 75 and some decidedly dodgy haircuts), would belt out vaguely recognisable versions of songs by the Rolling Stones and the Hollies. To the left of the entrance was the dart board and seating area where Jude would meet her friends every Thursday night - unless they were playing away.

She noticed that none of the team had arrived yet, and so, made her way to the bar to endure the inevitable long wait while Brenda the barmaid finished her conversation on the phone. Brenda was the kind of barmaid who felt no compulsion to serve waiting customers with any sense of urgency, whether the club was busy or not. In fact, to Brenda, customers were merely an inconvenience to be tolerated in between numerous fag breaks and phone calls to her friend Jean. Jude had often wondered why Jean didn't just come and work there too, seeing as they spent most of the evening on the bloody phone to each other.

Sure enough, Brenda was indeed on the phone as Jude approached the bar. She didn't acknowledge Jude's presence, but it was blindingly obvious that she knew she was waiting; on account of the fact that the phone was right next to the sodding bar hatch!

Brenda continued to 'oo' and 'really?' her way through Jean's scintillating account of the day's gossip, whilst Jude drummed her fingers none too subtly on the counter. Finally, she finished her conversation with a promise to give Jean a call back when she wasn't so busy – Jude wasn't sure Brenda had ever been 'busy' and she wasn't sure what the fuck else she would have left to say to Jean either. Brenda made her way, slowly, towards Jude.

"Sorry to bother you," said Jude, aware that her attempt at sarcasm was completely lost on the thick-skinned Brenda. "But could I trouble you for a Bacardi and Coke? – if you've got a moment of course!"

"I haven't stopped since I got here," replied Brenda with a dead pan expression.

Jude raised her eyebrows in mock empathy and waited eagerly for her drink. She noticed some of the other girls arriving, and quickly ordered their usual tipples too before Brenda took the opportunity to pop out to the smoking area. It did not escape Jude's notice, that Brenda was mighty pissed off at having to serve yet *more* drinks!

Chapter Three: Ruby

Ruby smiled at Jude as she joined her at the bar, accepting the offered drink gratefully and taking long, greedy gulps on it.

"You ok love?" asked Jude. "Bad day?"

"I've had better," smiled Ruby weakly.

The truth was, Ruby was beginning to lose sight of any day that had been anything other than; mildly shit, to the absolute car crash that today had been.

Ruby and Jude had an unspoken connection and, whilst Ruby knew full-well that Jude would listen to her troubles without any hesitation, she also knew that Jude's own life wasn't exactly a bed of roses and she really didn't want to be a burden. Ruby hated the kind of people who moaned constantly about their lot, hosting their own pity party at every available opportunity, and she was also aware that she was in grave danger of becoming just that herself. Besides, in her experience, when people asked how you were, they weren't really asking for a blow by blow account of your shitty life at every encounter. And what good would it do anyway? Unless they had a magic wand hidden in their skinny jeans, Ruby knew that *her* shit was *her* problem- as had been the way throughout her whole life. Unfortunately for Ruby, it had also been the case that most other people's shit had ultimately ended up being her problem too; from her alcoholic father, to her neurotic and self-absorbed mother, to her current 'boyfriend.'

Ruby stifled a groan as Jude linked arms with her, a friendly gesture designed to guide her friend over to their table, but a touch that hurt like hell.

Jude gave Ruby a knowing look, "Do you need to talk about it?"

"Talk about what?" said Ruby none too convincingly.

"You know where I am," said Jude kindly, "just don't leave it too long." She didn't need to add, 'like I did,' but the unspoken words were understood by both women.

Ruby winced as she sat down in her chair, not least from the pain but also from the memory of this evening's events. She was always surprised that Tommy let her come – for some reason he never objected to her darts evenings – God knew he objected to everything else she did. She remembered his stale breath on her neck as he'd grabbed her roughly from behind. He'd smelled of weed and lunchtime beer. She had tried to resist his advances but, pretty quickly, she had realised that he was in no mood for refusal. He had grabbed her roughly by her long ponytail, dislodging some of the carefully placed hair extensions that she'd managed to buy online at half price. He'd wrenched her head back, causing her neck to click as he did so. The arm that was causing her current discomfort had been forced behind her back. She had stifled a cry; she knew that Tommy got some kind of sick satisfaction from knowing that he had her in his control. He'd pushed her towards the sofa, cracking her shins on the wooden legs of the cheap hand-me-down seating that Ruby had inherited from the flat's previous tenant.

"Don't fight me, you bitch," he'd growled. And that had been the sum-total of his attempt at foreplay.

What happened next was the inevitable outcome of a lunchtime drinking session between Tommy and his mates. He took her none-too-gently from behind, his hands still twisted in her hair creating needle-like pains to shoot across her head. He had held on tightly to her arm, pulling it further up her back as he took what he wanted from her. Ruby had bitten down into the cushion to avoid shouting at him to 'get the fuck off me!' She knew that one word of protest could mean that this whole sorry saga would go on for much longer than a few short bursts of thrusting and grunting from him. She prayed that the little boy sleeping in the next room would not wake early from his afternoon nap and, not for the first time, fought the bile that rose in her throat – the taste of regret and self-loathing.

Tommy had withdrawn from her unceremoniously and wiped his dick on the throw over the back of the sofa. Ruby winced and pulled her jeans up from around her ankles. She had already glimpsed the formation of a nasty bruise on her knee, and her arm and shoulder hurt like hell. She didn't dare look at Tommy; even she wasn't a good enough actress not to let the utter repulsion that she felt for him show in her face. She kept her head down, her eyes deliberately averted from his, as she made futile attempts to straighten herself up and regain her composure. She had lost count of the amount of times Tommy had humiliated and abused her in this way, but it still left her physically and emotionally battered every time.

Growing up, Ruby had grown used to the succession of men that had 'visited' her mother. Her father meanwhile, had continued to drink himself into a stupor - in the local pub initially - but eventually on a bandstand at the local park, with a load of other drunks and social misfits, when his money had run out and the pubs had refused to serve the stinking and aggressive mess that he had become.

Her mother had pursued these 'visitors' not only for financial reward, but also as a means of massaging her fragile ego. Ruby's mother had an inherent need to feel pretty and desirable, both sexually and emotionally. She craved the attention of all those around her with a neediness that was draining. Inevitably, after every vacuous rendezvous, the feelings of rejection and lack of self-worth that her Mother experienced would be shared with the young Ruby, who would be expected to cajole, comfort, reassure and 're-build' her Mother before the whole futile process was repeated. In between times, her father would come home - drunk and bitter – spitting venom at his unfaithful wife and generally causing carnage in the house before retiring to whichever park bench he had just got up from to further anaesthetise himself to life in general. It was this wholly dysfunctional upbringing that had given Ruby a wisdom beyond her years and a yearning for something better.

Ruby had moved out as soon as she was 16 and, ironically, had fallen pregnant almost immediately to a man who had promised her the life she longed for. Predictably, he had buggered off before the baby was even warm in her belly and she was left alone; penniless and pregnant.

Ruby walked into her son's room, gazing lovingly at the mass of soft, black curls that adorned his head. His gentle breathing made her feel calmer and she was thankful for his blissful ignorance of her current situation. He slept with the contentment that only the innocent can manage and Ruby thanked God for that. She knew deep down that she couldn't maintain this situation for much longer. She may have given up on her own happiness, but she could not give up on the future happiness of her beloved boy, Reuben. He was the only good thing that had happened in her short life and she was determined to make things better for him.

If only it was that simple. Where would she go? She had no family and very few friends, having left school long before her classmates – besides they were probably all off doing what normal 18 year-olds do; like going out to parties and building a career, not looking after a baby in a tiny little flat with an abusive arsehole boyfriend. And, as Tommy frequently reminded her, "What self-respecting bloke is gonna want a single mother with no money, no job and a half-chat kid?"

Who *would* want her? Of course, it didn't matter one tiny bit to her that her son was of mixed race, but would another bloke want to take on another man's kid if it might be blatantly obvious that it wasn't his? And what did she have to offer anyone?

Despite all these feelings of self-doubt, Ruby knew that she would have to find a way. One thing was certain; she did not want Reuben to become aware of his mother's plight, nor did she want him in any way to believe that Tommy was any kind of role model.

Reuben started to stir, wriggling his little body under the Teddy Bear duvet. His opened his eyes sleepily, and a huge grin formed across his face as his eyes met Ruby's. She reached down into his cot and lifted him up, embracing him tightly. She kissed his chubby chinks - pink and warm from deep and peaceful sleep - and Reuben blew wet raspberries in return. She laughed as she lovingly teased him.

Ruby winced as Reuben clung onto her bruised shoulder, but she gave the boy no indication of her pain. She carried him into the lounge where Tommy was sat on the sofa, open can of beer in hand. He had barely acknowledged her, except to demand something to eat, and Ruby had replied without emotion.

Thankfully, by the time Tommy had eaten, the effects of the day's drinking had begun to take their toll and he had fallen into a deep and noisy sleep. Ruby had bathed Reuben and put on some clean jeans, before taking the baby next door to her neighbour – the one person who Ruby could count on as anything approaching a friend. Mrs Jenkins looked after Reuben once a week on a Thursday, so that Ruby could go to darts; and Reuben adored her. It warmed Ruby's heart to see how Mrs Jenkins fussed over the baby and she had no doubt that he was well and truly spoilt on his visits. Mrs Jenkins had offered to have Reuben any time Ruby needed her, but Ruby was reluctant to take advantage and therefore never accepted the offer beyond Thursdays. Of course, Tommy's mum had also offered to watch Reuben, but she was a cold, opinionated woman who was oblivious to her son's faults and who likely only offered as a means of interference and control. Ruby would give her solitary access to Reuben over her dead body and it was the one thing she had stood firm about with Tommy; despite numerous rows and vicious beatings.

Ruby had left her precious boy with his delighted babysitter, thankful at least that she could have some worry-free time with normal people, doing normal things – for a few hours at least.

Chapter Four: First Game of the Season

Ruby and Jude took their seats, now joined by the rest of the 'girls.' Truth was, the only person who bought the average age below about 65 was Ruby; with Jude being the next youngest member at 48 years young. The usual round of leg pulling, laughing and general high-spirited nattering ensued, with the darts almost being an inconvenience to the night's proceedings. As usual, Pat led much of the evening's entertainment; her loud, rasping voice, booming above the others. Pat was short, plump and fiery. Her platinum blonde hair was permanently scraped in to a high bun that sat on the top of her head like a donut. Her face was never without make-up and her nails were long and always brightly painted. Pat was loud, outspoken and took zero shit from anyone. She was of indiscriminate age – being reluctant to ever share her *exact* age – but she was definitely past retirement…her mental age and general energy however, were that of a much younger woman. Pat was a natural story teller and never seemed to have a shortage of stories to tell. Things just seemed to *happen* to Pat and she turned even the most mundane of events into raucous tales - accompanied by much effing and blinding.

This evening's tale had begun with a seemingly harmless conversation about her car breaking down on the motorway – what happened next could only have happened to Pat.

"I'd only just picked the bloody car up from the garage," exclaimed Pat, "bloody wankers!"

"Why what happened?" asked Jude.

"Fucking thing broke down half way up the M1!" moaned Pat. "I phoned the garage and told them that I was fucking fuming and they'd better bloody well get me picked up! They were supposed to have fixed the sodding thing."

"Did they come and get you?" asked Ruby.

"Well they sent *someone*; although he was about as much use a rubber bloody leg. Apparently, he'd come down from up North. He gets to me after about an hour, waiting in the freezing fucking cold, and sure enough he can't fix it. So; he winches it up on his truck and says he'll drive us back to the garage, so I can pick up a hire car, and get them to fix the problem they should have fixed in the first bloody place!"

"So, all good in the end then?" asked Jude

"You'd have fucking thought so wouldn't you?" said Pat raising her voice a notch. "The fucker only stopped half way!"

"What do you mean he stopped half way?" asked Ruby rolling her eyes and laughing at Pat's indignation.

"He stopped half way!" exclaimed Pat, her voice now approaching fever pitch. "We gets half way down the motorway, just at the sign for the Dartford Crossing, when he pulls onto the hard shoulder and says;"

"I don't do bridges!"

"You silly fucker!" I say, "What d'ya mean you don't do bridges?"

"I don't do bridges" he says, "I've got a phobia!"

"A fucking phobia?" I ask. "You can't be scared of bridges you daft bugger; you're a sodding breakdown service! And do you know; that fucker would NOT go any further!"

"What did you do?" laughed Jude, imagining the poor driver on the receiving end of Pat's sharp tongue.

"I drove the fucking truck!" said Pat belligerently.

"You never did?" laughed Ruby.

"I bloody did," shrieked Pat. "I told that fucker to get out of that driving seat and to move the fuck over or I would leave him on the side of the bloody road!"

It turned out that Pat had done no more than to drive that big old breakdown truck through the toll booth, arm out the window, with the terrified mechanic in the seat next to her, his head between his knees in an attempt to control a full on panic attack due to his bridge phobia and, undoubtedly, partly due to the deranged old lady now driving his truck! At their return to the garage, the mechanics had indignantly proclaimed, 'You can't do that madam,' to which Pat had declared, 'I just fucking did! Next time send me a fucking breakdown driver who can actually drive – or better still fix my fucking car the first time!' After which, she had left in her hire car, leaving behind a group of dumb-struck mechanics.

By this time, the girls had tears of laughter rolling down their cheeks as they tried to imagine little old Pat, in her truck, barely able to see above the steering wheel, whilst her passenger trembled beside her!

The evening came to an end after much shared laughter, more than a few drinks and, unbelievably, the girls being one game up.

Ruby approached the end of the evening with the same sense of deflation that she always felt when it was time to go home. If it wasn't for Reuben, she would happily never go back. Ironically, had Ruby known it, Jude felt exactly the same way; although why *she* bothered going back was beyond her – she didn't even have the pull of a baby to draw *her* back.

Chapter Five: Pat

Pat returned to her empty house, thankful at least that she had left the lamp on in the lounge. She hated coming back to darkness. She knew that the girls saw her as the life and soul of the party, they would have been surprised to learn that most days she struggled to raise a smile- let alone a laugh. She awaited Thursday nights with the longing of a starving man waiting for food. Her Alf would have taken the piss if he could see her now – "Cheer up, you grumpy cow," he'd have teased her. Truth was, Pat missed her Alf with an ache that was physical. He had been her sparring partner, her friend, her absolute rock. They had laughed together, cried together, bickered together – frequently – but they'd done it all... together. For fifty years they had shared a home, a life and the pain of never having been blessed with the child that they had both desperately longed for. Alf would have made a wonderful father. Steady, reliable, honest; a man of integrity. A man not predisposed to declarations of love, but a man who had made her feel cherished and protected. The man who had put the bins out every Monday, who had brought her favourite roses every Friday on his way home from work and a man who had put up with her vocal rantings with quiet and good-natured acceptance. Without him, she felt hollow inside, like she was a puzzle with a sodding great piece missing – right in the middle.

Pat walked through into the kitchen and flicked the switch on the kettle; she still had to remind herself not to get two cups out of the cupboard. She had moaned like bloody hell every evening when Alf had said – without fail – "You making coffee?" He'd used the *same* words, *every* night, at the *same* time, and the predictability of it (coupled with the fact that he rarely ever made the sodding coffee) had driven her mad. Every evening she had given the same reply, "Do I look like I'm making the bleeding coffee?"

before trudging into the kitchen to prepare his drink along with a couple of his favourite biscuits. She would give anything to hear him again, sure she'd probably give him exactly the same reply; but how sweet it would be to hear his voice.

It had been 18 months since Alf had passed. Mercifully he had not suffered, but she still struggled not to expect him to walk through the door at any moment. Everyone had told her that the first year would be tough, and after that things would get easier, but she was actually finding it harder as time went on. When he'd died, there had been so much to do; organising his affairs, the funeral. And there'd been a steady stream of people, checking in to see if she was ok; the first Christmas without him, the first wedding anniversary. But as time had gone on, the visitors had dwindled. Pat didn't blame them, she knew they had their own lives to live, their own families to care for - she didn't expect them to be wet-nursing her through life. She also knew that she only had to ask if she needed something, but she didn't want to be a burden. And so it was, after all the organising, after the initial shock and adjusting had worn down, that she was left with the stark realisation that he was never coming back. It wasn't the birthdays that caused the most pain – they only came once a year after all – it was this, the daily cups of coffee that had shrunk from two mugs to one.

Pat took her coffee through to the front room. She switched on the TV and performed her nightly ritual of 'removing the muck off her face,' that Alf had always teased her about. She knew she had been beautiful in his eyes and he would remain the love of her life until she left this world and joined him in his.

She switched off the TV, she couldn't watch any more of those vacuous fuckers in the diary room, crying because they'd just got caught shagging a house mate behind the pool house. Pat mentally chided herself for not being able to turn the lamp off in the lounge even though she was going to bed. She had always hated the dark, and these days even more so. Alf used to go spare at her for leaving the bedside lamps on whilst they sat watching TV in the lounge.

"Why have you got the bleeding lamps on if we 'ain't even in the bloody room?" he'd moan.

Pat's reply had always been the same, "Cos I don't like walking into a dark room, it don't look welcoming. Now stop moaning and eat your tea, you tight fucker!"

She smiled to herself. If people had heard the way they spoke to each other, they'd have thought it was awful, but that was just the way it had always been between her and Alf. They were totally themselves with each other, no airs and graces, just total honesty and love; true love.

Chapter Six: Ruby

Reuben was fast asleep when Ruby had arrived at Mrs Jenkin's house. He was wrapped in a soft, fleecy blanket, snoring gently, on her sofa. Ruby's heart swelled with love as she laid eyes on her precious boy and she promised herself that she would fix this mess she was in – if only for his sake.

"Has he been ok?" she asked.

"A little angel," replied Mrs Jenkins. "A perfect little angel. You're welcome to stay you know?"

Ruby knew that Mrs Jenkins was no fool. She had no doubt that Mrs Jenkins had heard the shouting and screaming that often came from Ruby's flat and she knew for sure that Mrs Jenkins had not believed the excuses she had given her to explain the black eye or the broken arm. Ruby was ashamed that she had lied to Mrs Jenkins; but she was even more ashamed of the truth behind her lies.

"No, it's fine Mrs Jenkins, honestly…but thank you," replied Ruby with a rueful smile.

The truth was, Ruby could only imagine what a real home felt like, but she knew she wanted one; and life with someone like Mrs Jenkins was a very appealing dream of hers.

"If you're sure love?" replied Mrs Jenkins, taking Ruby's hand and giving her a knowing look.

Ruby had looked away then and mumbled something about getting back. She didn't want to cry in front of Mrs Jenkins – more importantly she didn't want to chuck her foolish pride out of the window and take Mrs Jenkins up on her kind offer. Besides, how she could she even dream of staying with Mrs Jenkins? It would be about 5 minutes before Tommy found out where she was, and she certainly couldn't bring that shit to a kind old lady's door.

The two women said their goodbyes and Ruby cradled Reuben into her chest, still wrapped in his blanket, as she made her way home.

As she entered the flat, Ruby realised that the place was in darkness and the telly was off. She knew that could only mean that Tommy was out. She also knew that signified two very different outcomes. The first, and best option, was that he had got shit-faced, probably hooked up with another girl, and therefore wouldn't come home at all. The second option was, that he had got shit-faced, was having a nightmare trying to get home, and would therefore arrive in the early hours, drunk, angry and spoiling for a fight. The only problem with option number one was that she knew she wouldn't be able to relax for worrying about whether option number two was imminent – either way she would suffer yet another anxious, sleepless night waiting for a beating that may or may not come. Ruby didn't dare let herself hope for option three; that he'd got into trouble and was either dead or locked up. She wondered what kind of person she could be to wish another person dead – she was probably going to hell for sure.

Ruby laid her little boy in his cot, kissing his forehead, whilst he barely stirred in his sleep. She made her way through to the bedroom and flopped into bed, dressing herself in her warm onesie before she did so. If nothing else, it would not send any unwanted signals to Tommy if he did come home.

Unsurprisingly, Ruby had fallen into a deep but troubled sleep, dreaming horrible dreams that were fraught and violent. Her dreams often featured a whole mish mash of aggressive actions; being chased, being locked up and frequently, Tommy's face on her Dad's body or vice versa.

Ruby was awoken by a frantic hammering on the door. She sat up in bed, disorientated, and struggling to make sense of the noise that had disturbed her. She fumbled for the light, rubbing her eyes and smudging the remains of the night's eyeliner. She swore as she stubbed her toe on the bed as she made her way to the front door, which now sounded as if it was being beaten down. Ruby flicked on lights as she went, her mind whirring with confusion. What the fuck was going on? It couldn't be Tommy; he had his key surely?

"Keep the noise down," she barked. Just at that moment she heard the words – "Police! Open up!"

What the fuck had Tommy done now?

Chapter Seven: Jude

Jude entered her house through the kitchen door, the same way she had left. She could hear Dean snoring in the other room, telly blaring, the house lit up like a fucking Christmas tree! She sighed as she took in the mess in the kitchen – opened beer bottles sat on the work top directly above the bin, a lump of cheese left open and going hard, and the remains of a kebab wrapper coated in chilli sauce. Jude scooped the mess into the bin, half-heartedly wiping the stains and spills left behind. She was so bored of picking up someone else's shit. She made herself a cup of tea and walked through to the lounge, stepping over the trail of crap that had clearly followed her husband in from the kitchen! She didn't stop to rectify the chaos, she simply stepped over it, leaving the lights on and the telly talking to itself as she made her way upstairs. Jude reckoned the biggest saving grace was the fact that there was absolutely zero chance of Dean making any attempt to 'jump her bones' and so she, unlike poor Ruby, would sleep peacefully in her bed tonight. In fact, she'd be surprised if Dean even came up to bed at all.

When Jude woke, she was surprised to find a text on her phone from Ruby. She was even more surprised to discover that Ruby wanted to meet for coffee. Jude had to admit that she didn't know Ruby all that well outside of the Darts team, but she did know that her Tommy was a controlling fucker and she would be amazed if he let Ruby do anything without his say-so.

Jude replied to the text and agreed to meet Ruby at the little coffee house in town. The shop had recently been taken over by a really nice woman who made great cakes and who had installed a tiny play area in one corner of the shop – that way little Reuben could play with the baby toys whilst they chatted.

Jude threw her dressing gown around her shoulders and padded down the stairs. The lights were still on. Dean had no conscience when it came to his carbon footprint besides, he had done something to the electric meter that meant he could avoid the usual inconvenience of actually paying for electricity! Dean, it seemed, had gone out. 'Thank fuck for that,' thought Jude, relishing the peace and quiet.

As she made her way through the lounge, Jude collected three more beer bottles, a pair of discarded socks, an empty crisp packet and a half-eaten bag of peanuts. She threw the whole lot – socks included – into the bin!

After a quick cup of tea Jude had showered and dressed, anxious to be out before her husband came back. She assumed he was at the bookies and would therefore undoubtedly return in a bad mood when he lost. Again! Stupid bastard would never learn!

Chapter Eight: Ruby & Jude

Ruby was already waiting for Jude when she arrived at the coffee shop. Jude had a sense of foreboding that the reason for Ruby's call was not good. She hoped that bastard hadn't hurt Ruby again. Jude knew that Ruby would deny it till she was blue in the face, but there was no mistaking the tell-tale purple shadows that would appear under her eyes from time to time – ill-disguised by make-up – and Jude had definitely noticed Ruby wince last night when she had gently tugged on her arm. Gutless wanker! Wasn't Tommy Murphy the big man, beating up a girl half his size?

Jude knew Tommy's family of old. His old man had grown up on their estate as well as his father before him. They were a dodgy bunch, the whole lot of them. Old man Murphy had been hailed a legend after being sent down for 10 years for beating a copper to within an inch of his life. Truth was, the copper had only come out after a call from a neighbour who'd been terrified for Tommy's mum's life after Tommy's Dad had pinned her up against the front door with a bread knife at her throat. The injustice of it was that the poor neighbour who had basically saved old Mother Murphy's life, was blacklisted for being a grass. Mrs Murphy had sworn allegiance to her poor, 'wrongly accused' husband and had visited him in prison (undoubtedly because she was fully expected to whether she liked it or not) until he died 2 years later of lung cancer.

Mrs Murphy herself was a bitch of a woman, and she had gone on to raise Tommy and his three brothers – one of whom had followed his father into prison, one who had died sniffing glue up his nose at the age of 15 and another who lived in a caravan in his mother's back garden and who was probably gay but nobody dared mention it - like feral animals. Tommy had grown up exactly like his parents; a feckless, unprincipled bully. Jude prayed that Ruby would find the courage to rid herself of this waste of space and realise that she really would be ok without him.

"How you doing?" asked Jude. "Everything ok?"

Ruby look shattered; she didn't look like she had bruises which was one thing, but Jude did notice the support bandage on her wrist.

"I'm alright," said Ruby, none too convincingly.

Jude went to the counter and ordered them two large cappuccinos and two large slices of salted caramel cheesecake – sod the calories! She carried the drinks back to their table and sat down, turning to little Reuben in his buggy who was smiling and gurgling.

"Bless him! He's getting so big! Can I?" asked Jude, reaching down to unstrap the little boy from his chair before Ruby could really answer.

"Of course," laughed Ruby, "I'm not sure I could stop you anyway!"

Jude giggled and bounced the chuckling baby on her knee, revelling in his dribbly kisses and attempts to bite her nose. She was always amazed at how perfectly acceptable it was for a small child to cover you in their own saliva – not acceptable behaviour in any other circumstance! Jude longed for her boy to be this size again; how differently she would do things given the chance. But then you didn't get second chances in life; not if you were Jude anyway, it seemed.

"So, come on. Tell me! It's lovely to see you but I'm sure it's not just a social call," said Jude.

"I know, I'm sorry," stuttered Ruby, her eyes welling up.

"DON'T apologise," scolded Jude kindly, "It's fine, just tell me.

Ruby took a sip of her coffee, licking the foam from her lips, the warmth of the liquid making a soothing passage down her throat. She began to explain the events of last night; although technically it had been this morning.

She explained about getting home and Tommy not being there, and then described her confusion at being woken at

3am. She told Jude that it had indeed been the police hammering on her door, almost breaking it down. She had known straight away that this of course had something to do with Tommy - it was hardly rocket science – but she was genuinely in the dark as to the exact details of his misdemeanours. Tommy kept her in the dark about *all* of his dodgy dealings and, in truth, Ruby would rather not know.

"So, I think it's drugs Jude," said Ruby anxiously.

The police hadn't told her much, but they had given her a vague idea of the trouble Tommy was currently in. Apparently, he had been dealing for some time – hard stuff – and one of his deals had gone bad. There had been some kind of turf war, shots had been fired and a car had been chased, demolishing a local Off Licence and leaving a man in hospital.

"Fucking hell!" said Jude. "What a prat! The only good thing is, that when they finally catch him, he'll be out of your life."

"I'm not so sure," sighed Ruby. "He won't go without a fight, that's for sure. I've had two calls on my phone from unknown numbers already this morning, but when I answer, they just hang up. I reckon he's sussing out what I know before he makes proper contact."

"Do you think he's that stupid?" asked Jude, "…second thoughts, don't answer that! Have you got anywhere you can go; you know, somewhere safe?"

"Nowhere," said Ruby sadly. "I haven't seen my mother in years and I'm not even sure my Dad is still alive! Besides, I need their help like a hole in the head!"

"What about your neighbour?" asked Jude.

"I can't," said Ruby. "Tommy would find me in about 5 minutes and it's just not fair, I can't have him beating her door down, scaring her to death."

"But you *will* tell the police if you see him… right?" asked Jude.

Ruby didn't answer, but both women understood that you didn't grass on someone like Tommy Murphy unless you had somewhere very safe – and very secret – to hide.

"I don't know what I can do," said Jude regretfully. "I'd offer you a place to stay but Dean's a fucking liability!"

"It's ok," said Ruby. "I don't expect you to be able to fix my mess. I don't know what I expected really. I just wanted to talk to someone I guess – wanted someone to look for my body if I go missing…"

"Don't say that!" exclaimed Jude. She knew that Ruby was sort of joking, but she also knew that Tommy Murphy was a loose fucking cannon.

Chapter Nine: Ruby

It was just 24 hours since Tommy had crept back into Ruby's life. After hearing nothing from him for three days after the police dawn raid on Friday morning, Ruby had not dared to let herself believe that he was gone for good. She'd had an uneasy feeling that she had been followed when she had popped out to the shop and she had still been getting some strange phone calls at odd hours of the day and night; but no verbal communication.

It had been around 11 on Monday morning when Ruby had been putting the bins out, that she had felt an arm grab her from behind, swiftly followed by a hand that covered her mouth. Ruby had been frozen to the spot, years of bitter experience teaching her to stay perfectly still and to keep her gob shut. It had been only seconds before her heart had sunk at the realisation that it was Tommy and, sure enough, his menacing whisper in her ear confirmed her fears.

"Keep quiet you bitch, or I'll cut ya!" Tommy threatened.

Surprisingly, Ruby had almost stifled a laugh at this – some homecoming this was, eh? Other boyfriends came home with a bunch of flowers after a spell away from home – not Tommy Murphy. No. He preferred the more direct approach!

"You got anyone in the house? You said anything?" he growled, not releasing his hand from her mouth.

Stupid bastard, she thought. How was she supposed to answer with his fucking hand on her mouth? She shook her head as best she could, and this seemed to have the desired effect.

"Good girl," he'd replied and guided her, none too gently, back into the flat.

Fortunately, Reuben was sleeping and, not for the first time, Ruby thanked her lucky stars for such a contented baby. Tommy had crept into the flat, checking every room and partly drawing the curtains. Ruby wasn't sure how he had expected her to hide someone in their flat, which was roughly the size of a large cupboard – unless you counted the West Wing of course!

After his initial checks had been made, Tommy had demanded that Ruby cook for him. He spent the duration of his meal, jumping like a cat on a hot tin roof at every noise he heard and dashed to the window each time he heard a passing car. Ruby didn't dare ask him what he'd done – she didn't really want to know anyway; you couldn't answer awkward questions if you had nothing to tell.

Tommy informed her that he would be staying at the flat but that he would be going out when night fell to avoid suspicion. Ruby didn't know whether to laugh or cry – she wasn't sure her nerves could take much more. When Reuben had woken from his nap, Tommy had jumped up to get him from his crib and Ruby had fought the urge to wrench her baby from his arms. Tommy had always been unpredictable but until recently, he had shown very little interest in Reuben and Ruby was happy for it to stay that way – Tommy making an attempt at stepfather of the year, was a terrifying prospect.

They had spent the rest of the afternoon in awkward silence, Ruby feeling like she was walking on a million eggshells. He had not tried to touch her and, stranger still, had not hurt her in any way, but his silence was every bit as frightening. Tension hung in the air like a thick black cloud looming ominously overhead. When dusk began to fall, Ruby had literally felt like her very last nerve was frazzled, the empty churning in the pit of her stomach, and the feeling of breathlessness had worsened as the day had progressed. She was on edge; her senses heightened in anticipation of Tommy's inevitable eruption as the realisation of the shit storm he had created for himself finally dawned.

When Tommy had finally left for the night, Ruby had sunk to the floor and sobbed uncontrollably. Her tears were a mixture of relief and fear – relief that he had gone, fear for his impending return. She did not know when he would be back, all she knew was that it would be tomorrow, and she sure as hell didn't know what mood he would be in. She had almost picked up the phone to inform the police but had quickly changed her mind. Tommy would go fucking mental if he found out that she had 'dobbed' him in, and she knew that the police would not be able to protect her from him – despite what they might promise her.

Reuben had splashed and giggled his way through bath time and snuggled contentedly into her as she'd given him his bedtime bottle. She had sung to him, as she always did, and her gentle soothing tones had soon had the desired effect on her sleepy little man. She had laid him in bed with her that night. She knew she shouldn't really, but it felt comforting to have his warm little body next to hers. She didn't have to worry about Tommy coming home for now; but tomorrow was an altogether different story.

Ruby had been up for about an hour when she had heard Tommy's key turn in the lock. It was still early, and her neighbours were probably still struggling to rise from their beds. She had felt her body tense as he entered the living area; immediately she could tell he was in a foul mood. His eyes were blood shot and he had the beginnings of a beard showing around his jaw line. His clothes were crumpled – as if he had slept in them – and he smelled strongly of weed.

She raised her eyes to him, trying hard not to let him sense her fear. Tommy was like an animal; he could smell fear as easy as those fucking kids could smell gravy on the Bisto advert! Reuben had been sitting in his highchair happily smearing the remains of a strawberry fromage frais all over his chubby cheeks. Tommy had advanced towards them, Reuben had begun to cry – sensing the atmosphere with the weird kind of sixth sense that kids sometimes have – and Ruby sunk back in her seat. She kept her eyes fixed on Tommy, the sound of her baby's cries wrenching at her heart strings, but she daren't look his way, she didn't want Tommy's attention turned towards him.

At that moment, Tommy had lunged at her, grabbing her by the throat.

"What you fucking said?" he demanded.

"Nothing Tommy! I just got up, I haven't spoken to anyone," cried Ruby.

Tommy seemed not to hear her. His grasp tightened around her throat, pulling her up onto her feet. Reuben's cries grew louder. Tommy ignored him and dragged Ruby through to the bedroom. There, he forced himself upon her and beat her with a viciousness that was brutal; even for him.

Throughout the whole ordeal, Ruby just prayed that he would not knock her out. She could hear Reuben screaming in the next room and she just wanted to run and comfort him. She tried hard not to cry out, to resist as little as possible, she didn't want to fuel Tommy's anger any further. She just wanted to survive her ordeal and look after her baby. The thought of what might happen to little Reuben if Tommy actually killed her, was much more terrifying than any beating he could give her.

Eventually Tommy was spent.

"You make sure you say nothing, or next time it'll be worse," he growled as he left the room.

Ruby could taste the unmistakable saltiness of blood on her lip. Her face was bruised, and she could already feel the swelling around her left eye. Her pyjamas had been torn and angry red marks were beginning to form across her stomach. She flinched as she raised herself into a sitting position reaching gingerly for her dressing gown. Reuben's screams had turned to sobs and she felt panic rise in her throat as she heard Tommy go to him.

She ventured from the bedroom, doing her very best to remain calm and controlled. She caught sight of her reflection in the bedroom mirror and was disgusted by it. Her lip was badly split and there was blood on her chin. Her left eye was so swollen that she barely recognised herself and there was a nasty lump forming on her forehead. She quickly averted her eyes from the mirror; anxious to return to Reuben.

As she entered the lounge, she saw that Tommy had lifted the baby from his highchair. Reuben's eyes were red from crying and he looked distinctly uncomfortable in Tommy's arms. He began to cry again upon seeing Ruby enter.

"This is your fault," said Tommy. "Now shut the little fucker up and then get yourself cleaned up. I'm going for a lie down."

Ruby took her boy from Tommy's arms, ignoring the pain that shot through her side as she did so. She did not want Tommy to think she was incapable, and she was anxious to calm Reuben's cries – for several reasons.

Once in her arms, Reuben began to calm, his little body shuddering as his sobs subsided. He had cried himself into a frenzy and had now reached the point of almost noiseless sobs. She held him tight to her as Tommy left the room.

She rocked him and sang to him, paying little attention to the throbbing that afflicted seemingly every inch of her battered body. The realisation of the danger that she and her baby could now be in dominated her thoughts. Silent tears ran down her cheeks as she thought about the impossibility of her situation. She could not tell on Tommy – he would surely kill her. She could not leave – she had nowhere to go. She was trapped. Trapped, terrified and desperately unhappy.

Chapter Ten: Match Two

Pat was the first to arrive at the club on the Thursday of their second team game. She had been so eager to come out; to have some human company. She felt like she was turning into one of those sad fuckers on the 'help the aged' commercials! The poor old dear who sits in one of those God-awful chairs that raises you up to a standing position at the flick of a switch. The same old dear who looks longingly out of her front room window at the outside world, having not spoken to a single person for 27 days. Pat was so lonely she ached. She had taken to buying her shopping one fucking item at a time, just to give her an excuse to leave the house. The poor sales assistant in the co-op had been subjected to Pat's, "Isn't it cold out there today?" conversation four times already this week. Pat knew she had to get a grip. She was going mad rattling around the house all day, watching the sort of daytime TV that was destined to send her bleeding barmy and polishing her coffee table so often that it was in danger of wearing away.

Pat certainly wasn't going to be signing up to SAGA any time soon, and she certainly wasn't up for sheltered housing, but she knew she had to do something before she turned into a dribbling, muttering mess.

Pat saw Ruby as soon as she walked through the door. She was wearing a scarf around her neck and a baseball cap – she looked like a pre-pubescent hoodlum. Ruby approached Pat and smiled shyly.

"What the fuck happened to you?" exclaimed Pat.

Inwardly, Pat chastised herself for her less than subtle approach; but that was her, honest to a fault. Her outburst had mainly been due to the shock at seeing the state of Ruby's face. Sure, she had applied plenty of make-up, and the baseball cap provided an element of disguise, but there was no mistaking the swelling around her eye or the purple shadows that showed through her foundation.

"Walked into a door," smiled Ruby, sheepishly.

"I'd like to meet that 'door' myself," said Pat, a little more gently this time.

Pat called over to Brenda the barmaid – she refused to wait patiently whilst Brenda and Jean put the world to rights on their nightly phone call like the others did.

"Oi Brenda, we're dying of fucking thirst here! Any idea when you might be ready to serve us? – seeing as that is the fucking reason you work here!"

Brenda mumbled something into the phone and walked huffily over to the two women. She daren't argue with Pat – very few were brave enough to attempt that – but she was definitely *not* going to serve her with a smile!

Pat ordered drinks for herself and Ruby and took them over to their table. She noticed with concern how Ruby moved, and she was not too naïve to recognise the signs of a damn good beating. Her Alf had never so much as laid a finger on her and she wondered why some women felt that they deserved the kind of treatment that Ruby was clearly receiving. Pat knew that Ruby had no family and she knew that she had a baby, so maybe that was why she felt she couldn't escape whoever was beating the shit out of her. If her Alf had been alive, he'd have knocked the little bastard into the middle of next week!

It wasn't long before Jude arrived, and her and Pat exchanged worried looks as they sat either side of Ruby. Jude really didn't know what to do – she felt helpless. Pat and Jude continued to exchange banter with a forced joviality, in an attempt to ignore the fucking great elephant that was sitting happily in the corner of the room. They were both women of the world enough, that they knew their interference could put Ruby in more shit than she was in already.

The rest of the team arrived – *ALL* of them noticed Ruby and *ALL* of them kept silent.

Blossom arrived with her girlfriend Apryl. There had

never been a person more inappropriately named than Blossom. When you thought of Blossom, you thought of delicate, tiny, white or pink flowers that smelled of cherries. Blossom herself was more like a fucking cactus than a delicate little flower! She was every bit of 25 stone and about 5 feet in height – she was basically as wide as she was tall. She had cropped hair that was dyed alternating shades of blue or orange, and her entire body – including her face – was covered in the most bizarre assortment of tattoos ever seen. She had a line of stars running up both cheeks, a choker of thorns around her neck and a portrait of Elvis on her left shoulder. Her knuckles were adorned with the words 'STAY TRUE' (whatever that meant), and she had a set of angel wings across her ample chest that were basically just a black, smudgy mess. Jude had often spent time marvelling at the bizarre inkings that adorned Blossom's body – many of which looked decidedly 'home-made' and were practically indecipherable. Blossom's boobs were enormous and always 'free.' She liked to wear racer back vests and no bra, which meant her huge breasts swung around freely somewhere above her stomach, and more to the sides of her body than the front. Her nipples protruded shamelessly, and pointed due South. Blossom had very few inhibitions and often compared herself to the likes of Ginger Spice or Katy Perry each time she changed her hair colour. Jude was quite envious of Blossom's almost delusional perception of her own physical appearance.

Blossom's girlfriend, Apryl, was small, petite and surprisingly pretty in a 'timid librarian' kind of way. She was the exact opposite to Blossom; both physically, and in her demeanour. Blossom bowled into a room and filled it up – in more than ways than one – whilst Apryl just sort of tiptoed in and sat quietly in a corner. It had long been a topic of conversation amongst the girls about just *how* Blossom managed to get so many pretty girlfriends; Pat had rather unkindly mentioned that they had all clearly been able to see her 'inner beauty!' Recently, the addition of Apryl to Blossom's long list of conquests, had caused further teasing, in that she'd had so many girlfriends that she was now naming them after the months of the year in order to keep track! Blossom and Apryl had now been together for more than three months; an absolute Personal Best for Blossom!

The evening's match was against a team from the Conservative Club and there was a long-standing rivalry between the two teams. The rivalry was very little to do with the political leanings of either side and much more to do with the fact that the teams were very evenly matched in terms of skill – both boasting some really good players – and every match had been bitterly fought, and narrowly won. The labour club girls were currently the champions and so had everything to play for this year. The banter was mainly good natured, although often near the knuckle, and there were some fierce competitive streaks on both sides.

Some of the friction came from the fact that the Conservative Club girls were mainly the kind who Jude described as 'wannabe WAGS,' and who always arrived in a cloud of perfume, tarted up to the nines, and with pretty much *all* of their goods and chattels on display. A further fly in the ointment was the fact that one of Blossom's ex-girlfriends – Courtney - now played for the Conservative Club, having left the Labour girls when Blossom gave her the boot. Jude reckoned the law of averages said they were bound to bump into one of Blossom's exes at some point – in fact she was surprised they'd only crossed paths with one so far!

The Conservative girls arrived in their usual fashion – brash and boisterous – skirts barely covering their backsides.

"Hold up, I see the cunt farm's open!" exclaimed Pat none too quietly.

Jude almost choked on her drink at Pat's remark, "Sssh!" she laughed.

Ruby giggled, and both Pat and Jude were relieved to see her smile for the first time that evening.

"Hey Blossom; anyone you know over there?" laughed Pat as she caught sight of the dagger looks from Courtney being directed in Blossom and Apryl's direction.

"Oh, fuck's sake!" said Blossom, "I was hoping she wouldn't come, bit unlucky to have to play against your ex!"

"It ain't got much to do with luck love; not when you've got as many exes as you have!" laughed Pat.

Blossom laughed and put her arm round Apryl, who was sitting beside her looking distinctly awkward. "I can't help it if I'm irresistible!"

The match went back and forth, each side winning and losing a game in equal measures. Courtney had ramped up her seductive efforts and was now crossing and uncrossing her legs for Blossom's benefit. Disturbingly, Jude, Pat and Ruby were unconvinced as to whether she was wearing knickers!

"Anyone smell fish?" laughed Pat.

Ruby let out an uncontrollable laugh at this and, for the briefest moment, felt almost carefree despite the pain it caused her.

Throughout the whole uncomfortable, 'Basic Instinct' encounter (Courtney was certainly no Sharon Stone!), Apryl remained quiet and unreactive. Jude couldn't imagine Apryl *ever* spitting her dummy out; in fact, the girls had barely heard her speak in the whole time she had been dating Blossom. So what happened next, was truly remarkable.

The last game was the decider; with both teams needing this game to win the match. Blossom was drawn against Courtney, who proceeded to 'drop' at least one of her darts before every throw, forcing her to bend over theatrically in front of Blossom, displaying just what she'd eaten for breakfast that morning. Still, Apryl showed no reaction. None that was, until Blossom threw the winning dart, upon which Apryl leapt from her chair and literally flew across the oche like an athlete at the sound of the starting pistol. She promptly threw the entire contents of a Pernod and black straight over the head of the unsuspecting Courtney who let out an ear-piercing scream, as the drink, and ice, made its way down her exposed cleavage, leaving a blood red trail all over her now see-through, white top.

There was an almighty cheer from the audience as the triumphant, and not-so-timid Apryl, used a surprisingly loud and uncompromising voice to tell Courtney to, "Put your tits away and get the fuck away from my girlfriend!"

Courtney looked at Blossom, hoping for some support, but was sorely disappointed as Blossom was now doubled over in hysterics and blowing kisses at Apryl who, by then, had returned meekly to her seat as if nothing had happened!

Courtney stomped sulkily away to the toilets to try and rectify the havoc that the sticky drink had wreaked on her thickly applied make-up and the over lacquered hair, that was now stuck to her face in a most un-flattering way. Unfortunately for Courtney, no amount of pub toilet soap was going to sort that shit out! The Conservative girls left pretty swiftly afterwards; tails distinctly between their fake-tanned legs.

The rest of the evening passed in a blur of good-natured teasing at the formidable Apryl's courage, and the prospect of Blossom having acquired a bouncer as well as a girlfriend!

It felt so good to laugh, but Ruby knew deep down, that she needed to find a little of the courage that Apryl had and sort her life out. Tommy's current mood was worsening, his drug-induced paranoia was fast spiralling out of control, coupled with the fact that he was now in a shit load of trouble with the police, and Ruby knew, without doubt, that time was running out for her and Reuben.

"What the fuck has happened to that girl's face?" asked Pat as she and Jude made their way to the toilet.

"I don't know Pat," replied Jude, "But I am seriously worried about her and that baby. He's given her a good kicking this time, that's for sure."

"Little fucker," declared Pat.

"You know who he is don't you?" asked Jude. "He's Tommy Murphy; old man Murphy's boy."

"Jesus Christ, what is she doing with that arsehole? He'll be the fucking death of her. That whole family is trouble, she needs to get away from him – they never did have any morals that lot," said Pat.

"I know," said Jude. "But what can we do? Apparently, he's got himself in real trouble with the old Bill. She can't grass on him, she's got nowhere to go, and you *know* that little fucker would hunt her down if she did manage to do a bunk. I'd have her with me, but Dean's a fucking liability!"

"She can come and stay at mine," said Pat, secretly pleased at the prospect of some company and an opportunity to do something more worthwhile than cleaning her coffee table.

"That's quite a big deal Pat," replied Jude. "He's proper trouble that one. You sure you want that shit on your doorstep?"

"I'd rather have that shit on my doorstep than the death of that girl on my conscience. I'm not scared of the likes of Tommy Murphy. I've got a few secrets of my own regarding his Mother if I need them; don't you worry about me," said Pat.

"What if she won't come?" asked Jude.

"It's not up for discussion," replied Pat vehemently; and Jude knew that once Pat had made up her mind about *anything*, she was a force to be reckoned with!

Later that evening, Ruby had been asked to share a cab with Pat and Jude. She usually walked home to save money, but her body was hurting like hell and she was glad of the offer. She had thought it a little strange since Jude only lived a couple of streets away, but Pat had not really given her the opportunity to refuse.

The reason behind ordering a taxi and soon become clear once they were all safely inside.

"Now, I want you to listen to me," said Pat, "I want you to not speak until I have finished. We aren't blind Ruby, and it is clear that you have had seven bells of shit knocked out of you; and it ain't rocket science as to who might have dished that out."

Ruby opened her mouth to protest – more out of habit than anything else – but Pat quickly raised her hand in a 'don't bother to argue with me,' kind of way.

"I also know," continued Pat, "*exactly* who your boyfriend is, and I am here to tell you that I will *not* be intimidated by Tommy fucking Murphy. Now you *have* to get out of there girl – if not for your own sake -then for the sake of your baby. Scum like that will drag you down - if he don't kill you first - and then where will your baby be?"

At this point, Ruby began to cry. She was so tired. Her nerves were shot. She was exhausted, frightened, and in terrible pain. "I've got nowhere to go," she sobbed.

"Yes, you have," said Pat, a little more kindly this time. "You are coming to stay with me."

"I can't do that," said Ruby, her tears mounting both with the emotion of the past week, and the kindness of these two women who she only really knew from a weekly darts group; they owed her nothing.

"You can, and you will," smiled Pat. "I've got plenty of room, I rattle round in that empty fucking house, day after day, since my Alf went; if I polish that coffee table one more time, I'll go fucking mad!"

At this point, Jude and Ruby exchanged a glance. They had never thought of Pat as anything other than a carefree and tough old bird, but her joke about the empty house clearly hid some tough times behind her smiles. It was funny thought Jude, how you never really knew what went on in other people's lives. How nobody's life was perfect, how they all had our own shit to deal with.

"But he'll find me," said Ruby sadly.

"Yes, he probably will," said Pat, "But we'll cross that bridge when we come to it. You are not going to waste your life on someone who wouldn't give you the steam off his piss any longer; it's not up for debate!"

Jude and Ruby laughed softly at Pat's blunt description of Tommy, and Jude squeezed Ruby's hand, "Come on love, you know it makes sense; you can't go on like this."

Ruby sniffed, and winced as she wiped away her tears; a wince that did not go un-noticed by Pat.

"Little fucker," she spat, "If he touches you again, I'll skin his fucking arse meself!"

"When will I come?" asked Ruby, daring to allow herself to dream that she might finally be able to be free.

"I know you can't come right now," said Pat. "We don't want him following you if we can avoid it. Go home tonight, wait for him to fuck off out again, then leave. You won't need much stuff, just a few clothes and the baby's bits; I've got everything else."

"What about Reuben's cot?" asked Ruby.

"Now stop worrying," said Pat. "We'll sort it all out. Just pack a bag and come to me. It don't matter about *things* – that can all be sorted – just get the fuck out of there before things get really nasty!"

"I don't know what to say," said Ruby. No-one had shown her kindness like this her whole life. "You don't need this shit."

"You let me be the judge of that," laughed Pat. "If my Alf couldn't tell me what to do, I'm sure Tommy Murphy's got no bloody chance!"

The three women laughed at this; Jude didn't doubt for one moment how stubborn Pat could be if she put her mind to it!

"Now, I suggest you get a cab to the station and I'll pick you up from there," said Pat, stuffing a tenner into Ruby's pocket and putting her finger on Ruby's lips as she made to protest. "If you don't know my address, then you can't be forced to tell anyone. What time does the little fucker go out?"

"I don't know," said Ruby, "He's been hanging around during the day but going out in the evening. He usually goes out after tea, I reckon he'll be gone by seven, latest."

"Right, I'll meet you at the station at 8 O'clock," said Pat. "And don't be late, else I'll going fucking mad with worry!"

Ruby tried to find the words to convey the gratitude she felt, but Pat would have none of it. Ruby hadn't known that kindness like this existed in the world and she vowed to herself not to waste this opportunity for her and her beloved Reuben.

The taxi dropped Ruby off a few streets from her flat; they didn't want Tommy getting suspicious if he was roaming about.

Once Ruby had left, Jude hugged Pat and said, "Thanks Pat."

"Don't thank me you daft old bugger," laughed Pat. "I ain't helping you, I'm helping Ruby!"

"You know what I mean," laughed Jude. "I've a feeling you aren't quite as tough as you'd like us all to think Patricia."

"If you tell anyone, I'll have your guts for garters!" said Pat.

The two women said their goodbyes and Jude returned to her house, thankful that Ruby might finally have a place of safety for herself and her boy – she had been increasingly worried about her and had felt helpless – she knew that a relationship with Tommy Murphy would not end well.

Chapter Eleven: Ruby

Ruby collected Reuben from Mrs Jenkins and thanked her for her help. She was sad that she wouldn't see Mrs Jenkins for quite some time after tomorrow and she knew Reuben would miss her – Mrs Jenkins was the closest thing to a Nanny that he was ever likely to have. Ruby didn't dare tell Mrs Jenkins about her plan and she hoped that she wouldn't be too worried when she disappeared, but then she felt sure she could send a card or something. With any luck, it wouldn't be too long before Tommy got arrested and then she would be free to speak to whomever she chose. Ruby felt a building sense of excitement in the pit of her stomach. For the first time in years, she felt hope. Hope for the future. Hope for a future that she hadn't thought was possible for the likes of her. Of course she was nervous; terrified that Tommy would somehow discover her plan or stop her from leaving. And what if she couldn't make it alone? What if she simply didn't have what it took to live a normal life? But Ruby resolved to put negative thoughts out of her mind – if nothing else she owed it to Pat, for sticking her neck out on Ruby's behalf.

Ruby hugged Mrs Jenkins tightly and kissed her on the cheek. Mrs Jenkins had noticed how Ruby had flinched at the pain that such a hug had caused.

"I'll be fine Mrs Jenkins," said Ruby softly. "Please don't worry."

"Just make sure you are dear," replied Mrs Jenkins, "You know where I am."

That was the third person in one night who had offered their support to Ruby – that was more than the total for her whole life!

When Ruby returned to the flat, she was relieved to find the place in darkness. Tommy was clearly out on his night-time ritual of skulking in shadows, and she felt grateful that she may at least get a few hours of undisturbed sleep; although the enormity of what she was about to do was beginning to dawn on her.

Ruby laid Reuben gently in the bed beside her. He wouldn't have a cot, for a while at least at Pat's house, so she didn't suppose it mattered too much. Ruby looked around at the sparse flat, noticing its shabby paint work, stained carpets and hand-me-down furnishings. Not for long, she thought to herself. One day, she would provide a home for Reuben that they could both be proud of. One in which he could have his little school friends around for tea, or she could maybe invite a friend in for coffee. A home that was clean, safe and happy – free from the threat of violence or dawn police raids.

When Ruby awoke the next morning, she was aware of noises in the kitchen. Reuben was still sleeping. She pulled on her dressing gown, barely able to tie the cord, her arm was now so painful; she hoped it wasn't broken. Ruby made her way through to the kitchen where Tommy was opening and shutting cupboard doors, sweeping their contents to one side as he searched for something – Ruby did not ask what he was looking for, she knew for sure it wouldn't be anything good.

She went over to the sink to fill the kettle. She looked at Tommy, who had now become almost manic in his search.

"You ok Tommy?" she asked.

"You need to pack," said Tommy.

"Why?" asked Ruby, panic rising in her throat.

"Because we are leaving you stupid bitch," snarled Tommy.

"But…" Ruby made to protest but was stopped in her tracks as Tommy suddenly located what he had been searching for.

"I am in no fucking mood to argue," said Tommy, pointing the barrel of a small black handgun in Ruby's direction. "Now if you are not packed in five minutes, then I swear I'll shoot the fucking pair of you!"

Ruby was speechless; her stomach lurched, and she wasn't altogether sure if she was about to throw up or wet herself. Her first thought flew to Reuben sleeping in the next room. She ran to him, gathering him up into her arms...and then it dawned on her. All hope was lost. She wasn't going to meet Pat. She wasn't going to be rescued. She was never going to have the life she had dreamed of. Instead she was being taken hostage by a paranoid lunatic with a gun. A lunatic who was about to force her to live like a fugitive while he tried to out-run the law like Bonnie and fucking Clyde. A lunatic who was making her more frightened than she had ever been in her life.

Chapter Twelve: Jude

Jude was so pissed off. When she'd got in the night before, Dean had been entertaining a few of his cronies. Her lounge had looked like the meeting place for a local fuck-wit convention. The room had been thick with the stench of cigarette smoke, and empty beer cans littered every available surface. Dean had been loud and even more obnoxious than usual and was clearly playing up to his 'audience.'

"Make us something to eat," he'd slurred, showing his stupid friends just how masterful he was in his own house.

They had all cracked up at this display of apparent manliness - and had laughed even louder when Jude had told him to fuck off and make his own food! She'd taken herself off to bed and tried hard to get to sleep above the racket that went on way into the night downstairs. When she awoke, there was a random bloke asleep on her couch and Dean was snoring and farting loudly in his usual chair. The place now smelled of stale smoke, stale beer and stale sweat! She looked around her and wondered what the fuck she was doing with her life. Here she'd been, lecturing Ruby on being strong and not wasting her life on some useless tosser, when she was just as bloody bad herself. Her husband was a twat, her son was a criminal and her house was a shit hole. Jude didn't know who she was most mad at…them or herself. She guiltily thought about how she had reprimanded Ruby in the past for not leaving just because she had nowhere to go. Jude had nowhere else to go either, she also had no job; but she was fucked if this was going to be the rest of her life!

Jude ignored Dean for the rest of the day. She didn't rise to his incessant griping and moaning and was relieved went he went upstairs for a lie down because he was tired – tired her arse! He was hung over and he'd done fuck all for most of the day!

Jude couldn't help but keep watching the clock. She was really beginning to feel anxious for Ruby. She hoped the poor girl would manage to get away. She had told Pat to text her once Ruby had been safely collected; Jude was willing 8 o'clock to arrive. It was funny how recently, her whole life seemed to be flashing before her eyes, but these few hours had felt like an eternity.

At 8:30, Jude's phone pinged. She leapt on the phone eagerly, barely allowing the text beeps to finish. She held her breath as she opened the message…

"She's not here!"

Jude's stomach flipped, and she stifled a gasp. Fuck! Where was Ruby? Perhaps she had changed her mind? She didn't dare imagine the alternative. Jude replied to Pat asking her what they should do. Pat quite rightly said that what else could they do? But it was clear from her message that she was just as worried as Jude.

Jude paced in and out of the lounge; absent-mindedly tidying things away. She bleached the kitchen sink, cleaned the cooker top and put on a load of washing. She made herself a cup of tea and tried to sit down in the lounge; but she couldn't settle. Her mind was racing with the endless, but grim, possibilities of any situation that involved Tommy Murphy. In the end she could bare it no longer. She went through to the kitchen and picked up her coat from the back of a chair, just as Dean came down from his nap.

"Where the fuck are *you* going?" he asked.

"OUT!" said Jude, walking out of the back door without waiting for his reply.

She heard him holler something about his dinner, but quite frankly she didn't give a shit if he starved to death!

Jude wasn't really sure what she was going to do, but she knew she had to speak to Pat. She remembered roughly where Pat lived, although she wasn't certain of the exact house. She arrived in Pat's road and began to walk from one end to the other; somehow, she had a feeling she would sense Pat's house, although deep down she realised that was a ridiculous plan. She needn't have worried. Before Jude was even half-way up the road, a figure came hurrying down one of the paths in front of a house which seemed to have every light, in every room, turned on.

"Fucking hell Jude!" exclaimed Pat. "I'm going out of my fucking mind here! If he's hurt her, I swear........."

"Let's not panic," said Jude, feeling exactly the opposite. "She might have just lost her bottle," although deep down, both she, and Pat, were certain that something more sinister had gone on. They had both been sure that Ruby had finally found the courage to leave, and the possible reason behind why she had not met Pat was too terrifying to contemplate.

"What are we going to do?" asked Jude.

"Do you know where she lived?" asked Pat.

"I think so," replied Jude.

"Right, well let's go and have a little check…just in case," said Pat.

Jude didn't dare ask, 'in case of what?' but instead nodded grimly and led Pat in the direction of Ruby's flat. Jude needn't have worried about how they would find Ruby's flat; it was sadly, blindingly obvious which was hers the moment they approached the only small block of maisonettes in the street. Tattered curtains hung at the windows and the front room light was still on. The two women loitered about in the road for a while like Cagney and bloody Lacey on a stake out. Jude wasn't sure what they were waiting for, but they were both understandably anxious at the prospect of Tommy loony Murphy still being inside the flat for some reason.

When they had seen no signs of life, nor heard any sounds, they exchanged an unspoken agreement before climbing the set of stone steps nervously to Ruby's front door which had been left open – it seemed that whoever had been in this flat had left in quite a hurry. Jude and Pat gingerly pushed the front door open and stepped inside.

Inside was utter carnage. Drawers and cupboards were flung open with their contents strewn everywhere. There were a couple of smashed plates on the kitchen floor and a whole host of tins and packets littered every surface – clearly someone had been rummaging through these in cupboards in a desperate and hurried manner. In the bedroom, clothes were left in random heaps and a child's teddy lay forlornly on the bunched-up rug.

Jude looked at Pat who for once was speechless, her mouth open, her eyes filled with tears. Jude swallowed the lump in her throat; a mixture of total fear and anger. Anger for the bastard who had clearly left in a hurry and who had most likely taken the terrified Ruby with him, and real fear for Ruby's safety. …Not to mention the baby. Jude prayed to God that Tommy had not hurt them.

"We have to find her," said Pat quietly.

Jude nodded, but she had absolutely no idea how they were going to go about it. All she did know was that if they called the police and Tommy or his bitch of a Mother caught wind of it, then Ruby would be in even more danger than she was right now.

As they left the flat, Mrs Jenkins came out from her house next door.

"Is she ok?" asked the old lady, clearly worried for Ruby's welfare. Her voice choked as she enquired after the baby.

Pat and Jude exchanged glances as they tried to reassure Mrs Jenkins that they would do all they could to help Ruby.

"Do you know where they have gone?" asked Jude.

Mrs Jenkins shook her head sadly. She told them that she thought she had heard a commotion early this morning, but she had been too frightened to interfere.

"I feel so awful," said Mrs Jenkins. "I should have called the police, but I worry that will make things worse for her; she's a lovely girl you know. And that baby…"

Pat put her hand reassuringly on Mrs Jenkins' arm, "Don't worry love, it's not your fault. He's a wrong-un through and through that one."

Pat gave her number to Mrs Jenkins in the hope that she might find out something that could help, but none of them were holding their breath.

Chapter Thirteen: Pat

The week dragged by more slowly than ever for Pat. She was literally sick with worry and had barely eaten since Ruby's disappearance. In her heart, she knew that something bad had happened and she had almost decided to call the police on more than one occasion, but what could they do? To be honest, the police were already looking for Tommy anyway, so alerting them to Ruby's plight (which she couldn't really tell them much about as she didn't *actually* have anything to tell, other than a load of suspicions) would probably make the situation worse.; especially if Tommy thought Ruby was a grass. Besides, what if Ruby had simply decided just to stick with Tommy? Stranger things had happened and after all, she was a grown woman.

Pat had spoken to Alf's picture many times that week; she missed him more than ever. He would have known exactly what to do.

After a week had passed, Pat met Jude for a coffee. Jude was just as worried as she was. They chatted together about this and that, but the conversation returned many times to Ruby's plight.

"I don't know what else we can do," said Jude. "I've been past the flat several times this week – not sure what I'm hoping to find! I did notice that some tape had been put across the door yesterday, so I reckon the police have already poked their noses inside too. Do you think we should tell them?"

"I don't know," said Pat. "Part of me thinks absolutely no fucking way! And another part thinks that it's not like he isn't already on their radar. If we call them, at least they'll know that there may be a young girl and a baby in danger when they do eventually catch up with him."

"I reckon you're right," replied Jude. "I don't see how it can make things any worse for Ruby if we do tell them – that's if she's still in one bloody piece!"

"Don't say that!" exclaimed Pat. "I can't bear to think of what he might have done to her – Bastard!"

The two women finally decided to visit the police station in the morning. Jude had to be a little careful in case Dean got wind of her talking to the Old Bill. He would have something to say about it, that was for certain! Even if it was absolutely none of his sodding business and had bugger all to do with him, Dean would *definitely* have an opinion; and it *wouldn't* be favourable. Dean had a long-standing loathing of coppers; but then Jude reckoned that if you spent your life avoiding any kind of honest work and engaging in all manner of dodgy dealings, you weren't likely to be at the top of *their* Christmas card list either!

Pat and Jude arranged to meet at the shopping centre at 10 the next morning. Jude normally took the dog out for a walk around that time, so she had less chance of raising Dean's suspicions.

As they hugged goodbye, Jude realised, quite sadly, that Pat was the closest thing she'd had to a friend in years. A friend that was hers and no-one else's. She wondered if they would have become so close had it not been for their shared concern about Ruby - maybe not - but then fate had a funny way of bringing people together. All Jude knew was, that she was grateful for Pat's friendship. Pat was a decent woman. She was honest and loyal, she didn't suffer fools gladly and, in less stressful circumstances, she could be a right laugh. It was beginning to dawn on Jude just what she had been missing for so long. She had totally lost her own identity in the mixed sea of chaos and mundanity that had become her life; and she was determined to find herself again.

"I'll see you in the morning girl," said Pat hugging Jude in return.

Pat was growing fond of Jude too. It was ironic how the two women were beginning to find their way again through the loneliness that had slowly been eating away at both of them; for different reasons.

"You going to darts tonight?" asked Jude.

"Might as well," said Pat. "It won't hurry things along for Ruby in any way if we don't go. Besides, I don't want too many tongues wagging if none of us turn up. We can explain away Ruby, but you know what the gossip mongers are like... they'll have a field day if none of us go!"

Jude laughed, "Nosy fuckers! See you in the morning."

Chapter Fourteen: Little Dean

Dean Junior sat on the hard, plastic chair in the police station waiting room. It had been a long night. His head was throbbing from the copious amount of Vodka that was now beginning to leave his system, and he was pretty sure he was starting to rattle; the thought terrified him.

What had started out as a bit of a laugh, was beginning to take its toll on even his young body and, if the truth be known, he was beginning to tire of it all. Sure, he played the big man to his mates, but deep down he was starting to feel increasingly anxious about his current predicament. He wasn't sure whether his anxiety and paranoia were due to the heavy gear he was growing increasingly used to smoking – even he wasn't blind enough not to notice that recreational use was quickly becoming a daily need – or whether he really *was* in as much shit as he feared he might be.

Right at the very beginning, Dean Junior had been nervous about getting involved with the likes of Tommy Murphy, but his male bravado had not allowed him to voice his concerns. The last thing he needed was for his mates to think he was some kind of pussy. But now, here he was, on his own, without a 'mate' in sight, and possibly deep in the kind of shit that he knew he may never get out of.

It hadn't helped that shortly before he was 'asked to come in for questioning' – which basically meant, 'get yourself to the station willingly son, or we'll find a way to arrest you' – he had been having a long and emotional conversation with Chelsea; an on-off girlfriend who was now apparently carrying his baby! He was already on remand for a crime that was sure to get him some bird when it finally went to court. They'd throw the fucking book at him if this shit got out; he wouldn't be playing the dutiful father any time before the kid left school at this rate!

Chapter Fifteen: Emma

Emma looked around at her bathroom and sighed. There were puddles of water all over the floor, the tube of toothpaste – squeezed from the middle and oozing out – was discarded on the window sill instead of in the special holder placed directly *below* the window sill, and the two towels which she was sure she had only just washed, lay in a crumpled, wet, heap next to the bath. Bath time in the Webster household was always the same. Bathing three boisterous young boys was never an easy feat, and the mess they left behind was almost apocalyptic! But, as she mopped up the puddles and hung the towels on the radiator, she knew she wouldn't have it any other way. She left the bathroom and tiptoed into the twins' bedroom. They lay entwined in each other's arms, their blond heads touching, each snoring softly. They could never agree on who should have the top bunk and so, resorted to squeezing in to one small bed night after night. Emma suspected the 'bunk bed row' was just a smoke screen for the fact that they were inseparable and slept much better together. She kissed their foreheads, one by one, and her heart swelled with love for them.

She made her way across the small landing to Sam's room. He was sitting up in bed reading; him being the 'big boy' of the family at an impressive 9 years old. The floppy fringe that he refused to have cut, and was apparently the fashion nowadays, fell across his forehead. She sat on the edge of his bed and pulled him in tight to her. He was getting too big to hug her in front of his mates now, but deep down he was as loving as ever, and she knew he loved a snuggle as much as his brothers.

"Don't stay up too late now," said Emma. "Lights out at 8. Your Dad'll be walking through that door any minute and I'm off to Darts.

"Will he come up and tuck me in?" asked Sam.

"Course he will," replied Emma, ruffling Sam's hair. "He never forgets, even if you're asleep. Love you."

"Love you Mum."

Emma went back downstairs and decided to ignore the carnage in the kitchen – it'd still be there tomorrow! She had prepared dinner for Steve – her husband – and left it in the microwave; as long as he got fed and watered, he didn't complain about much.

Emma knew how lucky she was. Sure; their house certainly wasn't grand, and they spent most months robbing Peter to pay Paul, but they were rich in so many other ways. Steve was a good bloke; he worked hard and loved his family. Every time Emma looked at her boys, she felt blessed, no matter how mad they had driven her that day, and she loved her husband more now than she had when they had met almost 20 years ago.

Emma heard Steve's key in the front door and pulled on her coat. Thursdays were the only night that she went out and, much as she loved her boys, she really looked forward to her 'me time.'

"Something I said?" laughed Steve as Emma moved to pass through the door just as he came in.

"You're late," smiled Emma, "Sneaky pint on the way home?"

"I couldn't possibly say," replied Steve, pulling his wife in for a hug and giving her bottom a firm squeeze.

"I haven't got time for that nonsense," said Emma, planting a kiss on his stubbled cheek. "The kids are in bed, Sam's waiting for you to tuck him – but lights out at 8!"

"I'll wait up for you," winked Steve.

Emma smiled, knowing full well that Steve would be snoring his head off by the time she got back!

The Three Sisters

The Labour Club girls were playing away at the Three Sisters pub, jokily known as the Six Tits by locals. The pub was considerably posher than the Labour Club – although that wasn't exactly tricky – and *all* of the girls made an extra effort to dress up a bit more than they usually did... *All* of the girls, *except* Blossom that was, who wore her usual jeans and tits-free-racer-back-vest combo.

The pub was packed when they arrived, having hosted its weekly Jazz afternoon which was always well attended by the wealthy old farts from the surrounding area. Mobility scooters in varying colours waited in the front carpark for their inebriated owners to reclaim, as they made the mercifully short, but wobbly, journey home. The landlady had affectionately named this particular group of her clientele as her 'SAGA Louts' and, what they lacked in youthfulness, they made up for in sheer brass neck.

They were a lecherous old bunch those SAGA louts. Jude often marvelled at how they could get away with brazenly kissing and hugging - a little too tightly - any female under the age of 70 who entered the pub. If a bloke of 40 came up to you and started stroking your arm, and more-or-less rubbing himself up and down your leg, he'd have got a smack in the mouth. But these old codgers knew that their advancing years meant that they could get away with blue, bloody murder! They used the offer of a drink and a winning smile to mask their almost inappropriate advances; and who in their right mind was going to smack an octogenarian in the mouth for innocently offering a free drink and a smile?! It made Jude chuckle; crafty old buggers.

"They'd have a bloody heart attack if they got a reaction," Pat had joked on several occasions.

The SAGA louts never stayed much past 8 anyway. They stayed long enough for a cheeky grope, before staggering out to their mobility scooters, with a belly full of Pale Ale, and weaving their way home, to be tucked up and fast asleep in bed by nine.

The match got under way just after 9; the Six Tits girls arriving in their shiny BMWs and entering the pub in a waft of expensive perfume. Pat wasn't at all impressed by their money, she thought they were a bit uptight if she was perfectly honest; all boobs and Botox. Their world was a very different one to that of the Labour Club but, once you got a few drinks down their necks, they quickly started to lose their airs and graces.

Blossom and Apryl received a few raised eyebrows from a couple of their opponents, but Blossom never gave a toss either way. The match was fairly close, although the home team had some decent players. Jude and Pat both tried hard to join in, but each of them was thinking about Ruby. A couple of the girls had asked after Ruby, and Pat had given some vague answer about babysitters. There were always a couple of reserves who accompanied the weekly matches, and they were more than happy to step in and get a game to replace Ruby.

Emma approached the evening with her usual enthusiasm, pleased as she always was to be free of any responsibility for the evening. Emma drank with the gusto of a rugby playing pro and, not for the first time, Jude marvelled at her capacity for alcohol. Fortunately, Emma's game was always spot on, regardless of how many pints she had consumed, and tonight had been no different. In between throws however, she became louder and more ditzy than usual. She was well liked by the others, mainly because she was always so positive about life in general, and also due to her ability to relay the many mishaps she seemed to encounter in life without any embarrassment. If she knew she was scatty, she didn't show it.

This evening had been no exception. Emma had started to describe the time when she had decided to give herself a home bikini wax. Worrying about the possible mess to her furniture or bedding if she attempted it in the house, she had decided that the best place for the procedure would be on the back doorstep. Emma had dutifully heated the wax and positioned herself, knicker-less, on the back doorstep.

She had carefully warmed the wax in the microwave, according to the instructions, and had attempted to apply the hot, and incredibly runny goo, to the desired area. What she hadn't banked on, was the fact that she had left the waxing strips just out of reach on the table behind her. As she squirmed and wriggled on the doorstep, the wax had begun to solidify at an alarming rate as she tried desperately to reach behind her and grab the wax strips. The whole sorry episode ended with her completely stuck to the doorstep, half naked and terrified to move in case she ripped off her entire lady parts, let alone her bikini line. Fortunately for Emma, her kids were at an after-school birthday party and Steve was on early shifts. He walked through the front door to find his wife, on the kitchen floor, half dressed and stuck to the step, with her legs sticking out in the garden!

"Do you know that bugger took 10 minutes before he could stop laughing and help me," exclaimed the indignant Emma.

By this time Jude and Pat were crying with laughter at the thought of Emma's predicament.

"I had to go to the doctors for some cream cos I'd actually took the skin off me pig's eye!" laughed Emma.

At this last remark, Jude almost choked and spat out an entire mouthful of Bacardi and Coke, whilst receiving some disapproving glances from the Six Tits girls.

Unfortunately, the Labour Club girls narrowly missed victory and their opponents gave them polite, yet smug, words of commiseration. Both Pat and Jude had been grateful for the laughter that had provided a welcome break from their current worries, as well as a brief distraction from the trip to the police station that loomed, and which they were both dreading.

Jude didn't have the same dislike for the Police that Dean had, although she always felt uneasy in their company. Having a husband and a son like Dean and little

Dean, meant that the long arm of the law was never too far away, and she dreaded the threat of more newly discovered misdemeanours landing at her feet. She always felt a little guilty, despite having nothing to feel guilty about. She guessed it was kind of like going through the 'Nothing to Declare' section of customs; it made you want to loudly proclaim your innocence whilst making you look like you were hiding ten pounds of Crack in your knickers!

"See you in the morning then?" asked Pat, interrupting Jude's thoughts.

"Yes; I'm dreading it to be honest," replied Jude.

"We'll be alright girl, don't worry," said Pat. "We can't leave it any longer...just in case."

Pat didn't say what the 'just in case' might be, but both she and Jude felt sick to the pit of their stomachs at the possible outcomes of Ruby's disappearance.

Chapter Sixteen: The Police Station

Dean had been in a foul mood that morning, although Jude was beginning to believe that her husband only had two moods these days – foul, and pissed! He'd moaned at her for burning his toast (which wasn't burned at all) and griped about the amount of sugar that she had put in his tea – she'd put bloody arsenic in it if he carried on! She smiled inwardly to herself as she remembered a story her dear old Nan had told her many years ago about a friend of hers who had got so fed up with her husband's moaning that she had pissed in his gravy! The old girl had sat down to dinner, whilst her husband congratulated her on a decent pie with 'proper' gravy and had barely been able to contain herself. How ironic that the only time her husband hadn't been taking the absolute piss was when she had quite literally pissed all over him!

That story still made Jude smile. She wasn't sure what was more incredible; the fact that a seemingly innocent old lady had *actually* decided to pee in the gravy in the first place, or the mental image of the ageing housewife, in curlers and a pinny, squatting over a Pyrex gravy jug!

Jude snapped out of her inward daydreaming at the sound of Dean banging his fist on the table and demanding her to; 'fucking well listen!' She looked at him with a mixture of contempt and pity – contempt for the pathetic excuse of a man that he had become, and pity for the fact that he had absolutely *no* idea that she was planning to leave him just as soon as she could.

Jude grabbed her coat from the chair and swung it around her shoulders. At that moment, Dean leapt from his chair and grabbed her by the shoulders, pinning her against the wall, "Where the fuck do you think you're going?" he growled, frustrated by his wife's obvious disregard for his wellbeing.

"I'm going to walk the dog," said Jude in a voice so cold

that she barely recognised it as her own, "…..and if you ever fucking touch me like that again, I will cut your dick off and shove it down your fucking throat!"

Dean's total and utter surprise at the calm, but barely disguised anger, in Jude's voice caused him to loosen his grip. At which point, Jude grabbed the dog's lead from the hook by the back door and whistled for him to come for 'walkies.' Buddy, completely oblivious to the tension between his owners, but always up for a walk, jumped out of his basket in the corner of the lounge, and scampered happily through to the kitchen; tongue out and tail wagging furiously. Jude placed the lead around her beloved dog's neck and, without so much as a glance in Dean's direction, left the house.

"*That*...was the last straw," she said quietly to herself. This worm had finally turned; she was putting up with this shitty life no longer!

Jude arrived at the Police station minutes after Pat, who was pacing up and down outside like a cat on a hot, tin roof.

"You alright Pat?" asked Jude, completely understanding Pat's anxiety.

It wasn't that they were about to potentially drop Tommy Murphy in it so to speak – not that it was really possible to put him in any more trouble than he seemingly was in currently, through his own stupidity – it was more the consequences for Ruby that concerned the two friends. Both were terrified that they may never know what happened to Ruby or, worse, find out that something awful had happened.

"Come on girl, let's do it," said Pat, linking her arm through Jude's. "We can't make things any worse than they are now; and who knows we might just be able to help her? Either way, we can't sit back and do nothing."

Pat and Jude walked through the automatic, sliding doors, with Buddy trotting patiently behind them – just at the moment that Little Dean was being led from the interview rooms towards the front desk!

Jude looked at the son that she was beginning to barely recognise. He looked awful. He had bags under his eyes and a thick stubble had started to darken his face. His complexion was pale, and he was sweating, visibly. He looked broken and vulnerable and suddenly Jude, had she not been so surprised to see him, wanted to scoop him into her arms and whisk him away from the shitty life that he seemed hell-bent on creating for himself.

It didn't take long for a mixture of shock and guilt to register on Little Dean's face. "Mum?" he questioned, unable to make sense of the situation in his current state of sleep deprivation and feeling like death warmed up.

"I'm just here with Pat," said Jude quietly, not wanting to give anything away.

"Had my car nicked," said Pat by way of explanation. She was an astute old girl and life had taught her more than a thing or two about playing your cards close to your chest. Little Dean didn't need to know that Pat didn't even own a car!

"You ok?" asked Jude, not daring to wonder why her boy was here...*again*.

"Yeh Mum, no worries," replied Dean, rubbing his face wearily, and looking anything like a man with no worries.

"You home later?" asked Jude, tentatively. She had long given up asking too many questions about Little Dean's whereabouts – it was partly self-preservation for her to not know exactly what he was up to.

Little Dean mumbled something about staying with a girl. Jude didn't recognise the name - but then why would she? She knew fuck-all about her son these days it seemed, but it didn't stop her from caring; no matter how hard she tried not to.

Jude touched her son lightly on the arm as he shuffled past her, looking distinctly sheepish. For the briefest moment she felt him pause at her touch, but he did not return the gesture. Jude felt the tears well in her eyes as she watched the hunched shape of her only boy leave the Police station – he looked much older than his 18 years and had the posture of a man with the weight of the world on his shoulders.

Pat put her arm around Jude's shoulders and Buddy, sensing Jude's distress attempted to lick the exposed skin peeping out from her trainers as a means of comfort. Jude gave a sad smile at Buddy's affection and wished she could receive a fraction of such love from her son. She gave a loud sniff and swallowed down her tears, so grateful that Pat was here with her.

Pat, wisely, said nothing but she held on to Jude tightly as they approached the desk.

The encounter with the desk sergeant was not as stressful as Jude had maybe feared it might be. Pat and Jude explained their 'involvement' with Ruby and how deeply concerned they were for her safety. They explained about the visible bruising on her body and the fact that she had a young baby with her. They told the Police everything they knew which, when said aloud, Jude sadly realised, didn't account to much that could help. The sergeant reassured them that Tommy Murphy was well on the police radar and they were actively trying to locate him. Unfortunately, at this stage they only had circumstantial evidence and so had little to ensure that he would be put behind bars if they found him. The sergeant obviously didn't go into too much detail regarding Tommy's crimes, but it was obvious to both Pat and Jude, that it was for something pretty serious. The Sergeant hinted that drugs and weapons were involved, which did little to lessen the concerns for Ruby and Reuben's safety. It seemed that the Police had also visited the flat, as Pat and Jude had suspected, and they asked that both women let them know if they heard anything that might help with their investigation. The Sergeant was insistent that the two women understood that Tommy Murphy was considered a dangerous individual, and that they should avoid any involvement with him; whatever their concerns for Ruby.

"Well, no shit Sherlock," exclaimed Pat as they left the station. "I'm not sure if I feel much better or much worse!

"I don't think we've helped much either way," sighed Jude. "I'm pretty sure that Bastard's got her and if he has, she's up shit creek without a paddle! We can only hope that the Police find him soon."

"I need a drink," said Pat. She didn't usually drink during the day, but her nerves were shot. She hadn't forgotten the encounter with Little Dean and wondered what the fuck he had been up to. Poor Jude; she was a lovely woman and she hardly ever seemed to get a break.

Her husband was useless, her son was on a fucking collision course to prison and now she had the worry of poor Ruby to contend with!

"Fuck it!" exclaimed Jude, "let's get a drink."

Pat and Jude made their way down to the narrow path that ran along the edge of the river that bordered their town. At the end of the path was a nice little pub, with a garden that overlooked the river. Jude found a seat and waited in the garden with Buddy, whilst Pat went into the pub to order the drinks. She returned with a bottle of wine in an ice bucket and a wooden spoon sporting the number 42.

"I ordered us a sandwich too," said Pat. "Cheese salad alright?"

"Perfect," said Jude, realising she hadn't eaten properly for days, let alone hours. "Do I owe you some money."

"Fuck off!" said Pat, and they both laughed at her bluntness!

Pat and Jude sat pensively in the garden, drinking their wine and eating their sandwiches. They said little, both lost deep in thought. Deep down, they both knew that there was not much they could do but sit back and wait; and pray to God that Tommy was picked up soon. Jude had the added anxiety of wondering what the hell Little Dean had been doing at the Police station, having clearly spent the night there, but she guessed the answer to that question would also be a waiting game.

Chapter Seventeen: Ruby

Ruby sat on the uncomfortable seating that doubled as both a bed and a sofa in the sparsely furnished static caravan. It had been a week since Tommy had dragged her here; almost by her hair. She wasn't entirely sure where they were, and she wasn't totally unconvinced that Tommy hadn't been slipping something into her tea to keep her quiet. She suspected it was probably Valium but, in all honesty, she almost relished the numbness that it afforded her. As long as she was 'with it' enough to care for Reuben, then she would rather feel numb than fully aware of the desperate situation she was in. She hadn't eaten, her sleep was fitful, and she couldn't remember the last time she had washed her hair.

Tommy had been acting mighty strangely since they had arrived. Ruby remembered something about him visiting his Nan's caravan as a kid, but she had no real idea where that was. She had been so shit-scared when she had been bundled into the back of a car, practically at gun point, that the last thing on her mind had been where they were going. All she had hoped for was that he wouldn't kill her – if it hadn't been for Reuben, she would have almost begged him to put an end to her misery.

A succession of strangers had been visiting Tommy, usually at unsociable hours. They all looked the same - gaunt faces obscured by a cap and hoodie, nervous and shifty in their general behaviour - furtively exchanging money or small packages from tracksuit pockets with a back-handed gesture that stood out a mile. Ruby tried hard to leave the room whenever she could, tricky as it was in such a small space, but she never made eye contact or exchanged any kind of words with their visitors. Tommy often left the van at night-time, returning with the usual stench of alcohol and stale weed that made Ruby sick to her stomach. She had given up all hope of escape, and was unable to contact anyone due to Tommy having smashed her phone into a million pieces on the night they had arrived. The only saving grace was that Tommy had not beaten her since their arrival and Ruby guessed this was because he didn't want to draw attention to themselves. In fact, what had been more sinister, had been his forced displays of fatherly affection towards Reuben, or the way in which he had held her hand whenever they were in the company of other site users. Ruby had tolerated these public displays of affection with the apathy of a condemned woman. She left the van only to visit the site shop, and always under the watchful and oppressive eye of Tommy. The rest of her days were spent watching daytime TV on a small portable set in the cramped living area and doing her very best to look after Reuben who had been fractious and clingy.

She pretended not to hear the hushed phone calls, nor the references to the 'evidence' having been removed. In fact, Ruby was capable of little more than breathing in and out, and even that felt like an uphill battle.

Chapter Eighteen: Jude

Jude had met with Pat a couple of times in between darts matches, and the two women were forming a really close bond. Not for the first time, Jude wished their friendship had been born out of happier circumstances. They had both reached a stalemate when it came to having the faintest idea about what to do next for Ruby – the truth was, there was absolutely nothing they could do, except wait and listen out for any rumours on the local gossip chain. Unusually for her, old Mother Murphy was keeping a low profile and a tight lip about the disappearance of her wayward son, which probably meant that she knew exactly where he was. There was absolutely no way on Earth that Pat or Jude could have asked any questions; they definitely wouldn't have got any answers, and it would only serve to raise suspicions and put Ruby in more danger – assuming she was still alive.

Jude had made up her mind to leave Dean, but she wasn't quite sure *how*…yet. She had learnt quite a lot about Pat and how lonely she had been since Alf had died. Pat wasn't a woman to air her 'dirty laundry' in public and Jude felt privileged that she had chosen to open up to her – it was further endorsement of their friendship. If nothing else, it had shown Jude just how different people's lives were behind closed doors; the truth behind the smiles as it were. Few would have guessed the daily struggle that Pat faced from her jovial disposition and 'tough as nails' demeanour, but Jude figured that life wasn't easy for any of them. It also served to make her even more determined to find happiness. Jude was every bit as lonely as Pat, although for very different reasons but, unlike Pat, she had the opportunity to change things and build a better future for herself. All she needed was courage and a bit of 'grit,' as Pat called it. Jude had spoken at length to Pat about her situation, although she had been hesitant at first to unload her tale of woe. Pat had been a surprisingly good and willing listener and had also pulled no punches when giving Jude some wise advice. Jude realised that she was as much to blame for her shitty life as the people around her. She had fallen into her situation through a combination of apathy and a fear of any kind of confrontation. She had basically 'rolled over,' as Pat had put it.

Pat's advice had been a wake-up call for Jude, despite the tears of regret it had caused. Pat hadn't been shy of an awkward exchange and she had delivered the truth; no matter how brutal it had sounded. Jude also knew that Pat had done it out of love – albeit it, tough love. It also made Jude think about how quickly she had given up on little Dean; afraid to confront him, afraid to deliver her own measure of tough love to the boy she loved so dearly. Well no more. Jude was going to fight for her own happiness, and she was going to fight for her boy too; whether he wanted it or not!

Darts carried on as normal, with the team coming out on top as the league games drew to an end. There was only one match left to be played, and this was to be held at a social club on a holiday park about 30 miles away. The girls had decided to hire a minibus between them and make the most of the evening. Despite the shit storm going on around them, Jude was looking forward to getting away; any distance she could put between her and the Bunkers Hill Estate, albeit for a few hours, would feel like a holiday.

In the meantime, Jude had decided to sit down with little Dean and try to talk a bit of sense into him. He had come and gone a few times over the past couple of weeks and, on each occasion, he looked like his nerves were frazzled. Something was going on in his life and Jude was determined to get to the bottom of it. She suspected that the 'something' was bigger than the usual scrapes he had got himself into, and she was not looking forward to hearing what it was – assuming he opened up to her that was. She knew he had his trial coming up, she knew he was smoking, (or snorting), some pretty serious gear; but this was more than that. Call it a mother's intuition, but Jude sensed that her boy had sailed up shit creek minus his paddle and she'd be buggered if she would let him go down without a fight. She wanted more than an existence for Dean Junior; she wanted him to have a life.

Chapter Nineteen: Chelsea

Chelsea looked at herself in the full-length mirror propped up against the wall in her bedsit. The room was sparsely furnished but it was clean and tidy. She smoothed the tunic top down over her leggings that were beginning to strain against her expanding waistline. She turned to the side, stroking her belly protectively. She wanted this baby to have something she had never had – a mother that loved her, and a family. A proper family. Chelsea had grown up in various homes throughout her 17 years and had known that she was a burden in all of them. Her mother had died of an overdose when she was just a kid and she had been pushed from pillar to post ever since. Her Nan had taken her in for a while, but when she died after a grim battle with lung cancer, Chelsea had been taken in by various 'Aunts' and 'Uncles' whose battle to keep her out of care had been more to do with the prospect of child support than any kind of love.

In most of the places, she had been tolerated and, in the less favourable ones, she had been treated little better than a slave. She had been used in all manner of dodgy dealings, usually involving drugs, where a child might escape suspicion. Chelsea had never succumbed to the temptation to fill her veins full of shit, having seen the destruction that it had wreaked around her. In fact, the only 'favour' her guardians had done her, was to make her determined not to follow their example. As soon as she had turned sixteen, she had taken off into the night with only a carrier bag full of clothes and a few hundred quid that she had managed to sneak away from the unsuspecting adults in her life over many months. Chelsea had been planning her escape for as long as she could remember and had used her wits to keep a little back for herself at every opportunity. She had always been careful not to take too much, in order to avoid suspicion. She had been patient – she had played the long game.

Chelsea had got herself a job at the local supermarket and had enrolled on a photography course at the nearby college. Chelsea had always been creative and knew she had a real flair for photography. It was her dream to one day run her own business, taking beautiful photographs and selling them for money; and she was determined to follow her dream.

Pregnancy hadn't been on her agenda, but now that the baby was growing inside her, Chelsea knew that she would do everything in her power to give her baby the life it deserved. Sure, it made things more complicated, but then 'complicated' seemed to follow her around like the grim reaper.

When Chelsea had first met Dean, she had been wary of getting involved with him. She knew he was one of the would-be gangsters on the estate, and she needed that shit in her life like she needed a hole in the head. She had rebuffed his naïve attempts to woo her and had told him in no uncertain terms that she wasn't into drugs or crime; and he was into both. Eventually, she had succumbed to 'coffee.' She had thought it was quite a sweet gesture since 'coffee' was seriously uncool for an aspiring rude boy, and she knew that he had only offered because he knew she would like it. Surprisingly, they had got on really well and had talked for hours. Underneath his tough exterior, Dean was actually a nice lad, and Chelsea felt that he had just kind of lost his way; drifting into his gangster life because it was what boys did on the Bunker's Hill Estate.

They had eventually begun seeing each other and one thing had inevitably led to another. Dean had pleaded with Chelsea to let him move in with her on more than one occasion, but Chelsea had stood her ground. She had told him that unless he got a job and gave up drugs and crime, then he would not be living with her any time soon. Of course, when she had told him about the baby, he had immediately assumed that she would take him in; but

Chelsea had remained firm despite her love for him. If anything, it had made her more determined; there was no way she wanted any baby of hers to be brought up with a drug taking father. Either he sorted his shit out, or she would do it alone.

Chelsea had thought long and hard about her decision to visit Dean's mum, Jude. She very much doubted that Dean had told her about the baby. From what she could gather, he had got himself into the kind of trouble that was causing him to wake up in the night in a cold sweat. Chelsea didn't really want to know the full details; sometimes ignorance was bliss. She did, however, want to at least give her baby the chance of an extended family. Chelsea knew that there was a likely chance that Dean would be going to prison, and she had resigned herself to the prospect of raising her child alone; support from a doting Nanna would be a dream come true. Dean had spoken about his Mum on several occasions, in a stroppy teenager kind of way, but Chelsea believed that deep down he loved his Mum and felt guilty for the fact that he become a bit of a twat. His father sounded like a total waste of space, but his Mum sounded pretty alright actually. Chelsea figured that she would at least be interested in the fact that her son was about to become a father; whether she would want to be involved or not, remained to be seen.

Chelsea took one last look at her reflection, smoothing the long brown ponytail that hung down her back. She had applied just a touch of make-up to accentuate her pretty features, but in no way did she want to look 'tarty.' She walked over to the small kitchen area and took the flowers from the sink. She wondered if she might be wearing them later, but she felt rude to turn up with nothing. Mind you, a bunch of flowers could be deemed inappropriate for the …'hi I'm your son's on-off girlfriend and soon-to-be mother of your unborn grandchild'… announcement that she was about to make. Dean's mother probably had little knowledge of Chelsea's existence, let alone formed any kind of bond with her, so she may not receive the news with the kind of enthusiasm that Chelsea hardly dared hoped for.

"Fuck it!" said Chelsea to herself. This baby was happening whether Jude wanted to be involved or not and she at least had the right to know about it.

Chapter Twenty: Jude

Ever since Jude had decided to confront Dean, she had not seen hide nor hair of him; she hoped he was ok. Dean senior had gone out to the bookies and would be unlikely to return for several hours – if he won, he would go to the pub to celebrate, if he lost, he would go to the pub to commiserate. Either way, Jude was just glad he was out of the house. She had given up trying to have any kind of conversation with him. He had become more objectionable than usual upon the realisation that his wife no longer gave a flying fuck, and he was becoming increasingly frustrated by his failed attempts to provoke a reaction. Jude felt the kind of calmness experienced by one who knew that the fight was over; and she was definitely not the defeated party.

Jude sat down at the kitchen table, a mug of tea between her hands. She allowed her mind to wander onto the way she would decorate her new little home. She didn't care if it was small, just so long as it was pretty. She had already begun to apply for jobs secretly, using Pat's address for correspondence. She hadn't worked in years and had needed to be more than a little creative on her CV, but she felt more optimism than she had done in years.

The doorbell interrupted her thoughts and Buddy awoke from his nap at her feet, giving a half-hearted bark at the unwelcome intrusion. Jude got up from her seat and made her way to the front door, puzzled as to who could be there. In her experience, a knock at their door usually brought bad news of one kind or another.

Jude opened the door to see a young girl standing before her, almost obscured behind an enormous bunch of flowers. She looked young – maybe 16 or so – and very nervous. Her face was pretty; large, dark, almond-shaped eyes, full lips and high cheekbones. Her skin was smooth, in the way that only young skin can be, and her long dark hair was tied in a neat ponytail, a few tendrils escaping to frame her face. Jude had absolutely no idea who she was.

"Hi. I'm Chelsea. I mean I'm Dean's girlfriend. Well sort of..." the girl stammered, seemingly at a loss for exactly the right words.

Jude smiled at her, feeling sympathy for the young girl's obvious nervousness. She had automatically assumed that the girl had meant she was Dean junior's girlfriend – a wry smile escaped Jude's lips at the prospect of her husband running off with a girl young enough to be his daughter. Even a teenager wouldn't be gullible enough to think that Dean Senior was any kind of catch!

A few thoughts raced through Jude's mind as she tried to make sense of Chelsea's appearance at her door. Why would Dean's girlfriend feel the need to introduce herself to his Mum when Dean clearly hadn't felt the need to share his news? As Chelsea reached her arms forward to offer Jude the bunch of flowers, Jude's second thoughts were realised. The young girl's slight frame made the small bump that protruded in front of her all the more prominent, and Jude quickly realised why she was here.

The girl quickly retracted the flowers as she saw Jude's eyes dart to her belly; almost using them to shield the truth. The two women eyed each other for a few seconds – each unsure as to how the conversation should progress.

Jude broke the silence. "I think I can guess why you're here. Would you like to talk?"

Chelsea nodded with relief, grateful that Jude had made the first move.

"I bought you these," said Chelsea offering the flowers once more in Jude's direction. "I don't know why, really. Seems a bit weird now. I don't know...I just thought..." Chelsea broke off wondering what the bloody hell she *had* thought.

Jude smiled. "It was a very nice thought; however weird! Besides, the last time someone bought me flowers, I was in a similar predicament to the one you're in now!"

Chelsea almost laughed with relief – thank God Dean's mother didn't appear to be a total bitch!

"You shouldn't have spent all your money on me, but they are gorgeous," Jude continued. "Now I would invite you in, but the place is a total shit-hole and there is no way I want Dean's Dad to know you're here! He'll probably be gone for hours, but I don't want to risk it. Let me put these in the kitchen and we'll go out for a coffee – Buddy could do with a walk anyway."

Chelsea stood on the doorstep whilst Jude put the flowers away and rounded up Buddy, who was indeed happy to go for a walk!

Once Jude was ready, she guided Chelsea in the direction of the local park. There was a coffee shop on the edge of the park and Jude bought two large cappuccinos and two lemon muffins; refusing to allow Chelsea to pay for either. Chelsea thought sadly that, even if Jude wanted nothing to do with her or her grandchild, she had been kinder to Chelsea in a few short minutes than anyone else had been in years.

"How far along are you?" asked Jude, cutting to the chase once the two women were settled on a bench at the edge of the park. Buddy ran around in front of them, his tail wagging furiously as he bought them stick after stick, to throw for him.

"Four months I think," said Chelsea. "I wasn't sure for a while, but I've done a couple of tests now. I've got an appointment at the doctors next week. I put it off for a while to be honest – bit scared, going on my own."

"What did Dean say?" asked Jude.

"Thank you for not asking if I'm sure it's his," said Chelsea, her eyes welling up. "I'm not a slut you know."

"I don't know why," said Jude, "but I'm sure you aren't."

Maybe it was the way Chelsea held herself, or the thoughtful gesture of the flowers, or the fact that she had actually had the bottle to come and face Jude on her own; but Jude felt sure that Chelsea was a decent girl.

"Does Dean want the baby?" said Jude, building on her earlier question.

"Yes, I think so," said Chelsea. "But, I don't know. We are both a bit young, it wasn't really my plan. But I can't have him with me until he…well…you know…"

"…Sorts his fucking life out," Jude interjected, guessing what Chelsea was struggling to say.

"Exactly," laughed Chelsea. "I know he's your boy and that, but I don't want to be around drugs and crime…you know...I mean, I hope you knew?"

"Don't worry," said Jude. "I know that he's got himself into more than a bit of grief lately and I think you and I could work together maybe, make him grow up a bit?"

At this point, Chelsea burst into tears. The pent-up emotions of the past few months, the realisation that she was pregnant at 17 with no family to help her, the anxiety she had felt before coming to meet Jude, not to mention the worry of little Dean's troubles, had finally got the better of her.

Jude grabbed hold of Chelsea and hugged her tightly.

"Don't worry, it'll be ok. I mean Dean may not want to be a father, you must understand that, but I promise I will help you.

At this point Chelsea sobbed harder, wiping a rather unattractive mixture of snot and tears all over Jude's shoulder! What a great impression to make this was!

"I'm sorry," said Chelsea. "No-one's ever really helped me before."

Jude hugged her tighter feeling sorry for this poor young girl; the mother of her future grandchild!

Once Chelsea had stopped crying and had managed to wipe away the worst of the carefully applied makeup that was now running halfway down her face on the serviettes from the coffee shop, she and Jude talked at length about their current predicament.

Jude wondered why she didn't feel more upset about Chelsea's news. It wasn't ideal for your barely grown boy to have got his very young girlfriend pregnant, especially when he was on remand for burglary; but then Jude figured, in amongst all the crap that had happened recently, maybe a baby was good news? Maybe, it symbolised hope – a new life, a new beginning almost?

The one thing Jude was entirely grateful for was that Chelsea seemed to have her head screwed on. She was glad that she hadn't given into little Dean and allowed him to move in with her – even a young girl like Chelsea was capable of tough love it seemed. Jude felt that Chelsea had done exactly the right thing and, if Dean chose not to take a better path for his life then sadly, Chelsea and the baby would be better off without him. Jude realised she should have done that with Dean Senior, years ago.

Jude became quite emotional as Chelsea explained about her life and the lack of love that had filled it, and it only served to make Jude have even more respect for the wisdom and strength of character that such a young girl possessed. Chelsea didn't talk about her life in a 'feel sorry for me' kind of way, but more in the words of someone who had clearly chosen not to be broken by her experiences.

Jude's mind flitted back to Ruby and she hoped, if they did manage to find her safely, that Chelsea could be a friend to her. Ruby could do with someone like Chelsea, who would understand, but would also give Ruby the gentle push that Jude felt she could do with.

Jude agreed to go to the doctor's appointment with Chelsea, and also gave Chelsea her number. They agreed that Chelsea would ring Jude once she knew where little Dean was going to be. Jude needed more than ever, to speak to her son. She wanted to know what was going on in his life and she also wanted him to know that she was there to help him – if only he would let her.

Chapter Twenty-One: Girls on Tour

"Fucking hell!" exclaimed Pat once Jude had filled her in with the events of the past week. "You sure you're ready to be a Granny?!"

"Not in the slightest!" laughed Jude, "But I haven't got a lot of choice really have I?"

"You spoke to Dean yet?" asked Pat.

"Which one?" sighed Jude, wishing for the hundredth time in her life that she hadn't allowed Dean Senior to talk her into naming their boy after him. "If you mean the waste-of-space I am married to, then no fucking way! – I definitely do NOT want him putting his two, fucking penny-worth in. As for little Dean, I haven't seen him all week," she added sadly, hoping that he was ok. He hadn't seen Chelsea either and they were both worried about the trouble he might have got himself into.

"He'll turn up," said Pat kindly, sensing her friend's anxiety. "Maybe just needs a bit of time to let things sink in."

"I hope so," said Jude. "Now let's stop all this doom and gloom for a day or two at least. What time's the minibus coming?"

The two women were sat in Pat's front room, their overnight bags packed at their feet, waiting for the minibus to pick them up for their 'darts jolly,' as it was now known.

"Should be here in five," said Pat, making a last few minute checks in her house. Jude didn't think she had ever met anyone who had so many lights burning in one house even during the day – it was like Blackpool sodding illuminations in there!

"I'm so excited," said Jude, feeling like a schoolgirl on her first trip away. "I can't remember the last time I went anywhere; let alone AWAY!"

"You dozy bugger," said Pat smiling, but secretly feeling every bit as excited as Jude. There had been so much sadness in their lives, especially lately, and they were more than ready for a bit of a break

The minibus beeped outside, and Pat and Jude jumped up simultaneously. Pat turned off an extra lamp that she had somehow missed, and they made their way out to the bus. Pat's house had been the last pick-up and the bus was already loaded with the rest of the team and their copious luggage.

"Christ!" exclaimed Pat. "We're only going for the bloody night!"

"Oh, shut up and get in!" yelled Emma, holding up a bottle of Prosecco that was already half drunk.

Jude saw the long-suffering minibus driver roll his eyes at his rowdy passengers – he'd be glad to offload them this evening!

As the bus set off, Emma poured out two more glasses of fizz for Pat and Jude, slopping a fair bit of it on the floor. Blossom offered to lick it up which led to raucous laughter from the rest of the bus and a rather rude reference to 'clunge-neck' and Blossom's sexual preferences! Apryl, as usual, just blushed and said nothing!

Mercifully, it was quite a short journey to the holiday park. Jude wondered how any of them were ever going to see the dartboard at this rate, but she was having such a laugh she couldn't have cared less if they won or lost.

The 'holiday park' – if you could call it that – was dingy to say the least. It was only a small park in comparison to others, as it was located in a run-down seaside town that was hardly a Mecca for discerning tourists. The plan was, for the girls to find their respective caravans and then meet in the bar once they had dumped their bags. They had all agreed to get ready before they left to avoid wasting valuable drinking time!

Pat and Jude were sharing the only two-berth caravan on the park and Jude was mighty grateful that she had such a close friendship with Pat – poor Sarah was having to share with Blossom and Apryl! There were 9 women in their group and, due to availability, there were two four-berth caravans and one two-berth. Everyone in the group was pretty much paired off in terms of friends, apart from Sarah who didn't come to darts every week and therefore chatted to everyone equally. Because of this, she was taking the 'odd' place in Blossom and Apryl's van. Technically, no one else was bringing their partners but Apryl was now so much part of the group, that no-one had questioned the fact that she was joining them. Jude did not envy Sarah having to listen to Blossom's nighttime antics – she might suggest ear plugs and a large amount of Vodka!

Pat and Jude opened the door to their van and immediately started laughing – it was absolutely fucking hideous! The cushion covers, curtains and carpets were all heavily adorned in strongly opposing patterns, the furniture was covered in imitation beech wood Formica that was peeling at the edges and there was the distinct smell of damp in the air. They walked through the cramped corridor to the tiny little bedroom in which twin beds were separated by a badly fitted shelf. A lamp – minus its shade – sat on the shelf and two thin curtains that were barely strips of material hung limply at the window.

"Bloody hell! It looks just like my house!" laughed Jude.

Pat laughed harder at this remark, "Welcome to paradise! Now let's get pissed!"

A few moments later, Pat and Jude made their way across the park to the clubhouse where the rest of the girls were waiting for them – they certainly hadn't wasted any time unpacking!

The club house was shittier than the accommodation – if that was at all possible – but none of them were too bothered. The drinks began to flow, and the girls became more and more animated. Apparently, tonight was Elvis tribute night at the clubhouse, and this caused a cheer of approval. The dartboard was at the back of the cavernous room and the girls were clearly able to see, and hear, the evening's 'entertainment' whilst they played.

Fortunately, the opposition were in just as high spirits as the labour club girls and nobody seemed to be taking the darts too seriously – they had all clearly relished the chance of a night out as much as each other. Jude was amazed that any of them were able to hit the board, let alone score.

The MC announced the first Elvis, who was considerably shorter, and wider, than his idol. He appeared onto the small stage; a vision in a white jump suit, straining across his ample belly, and decorated with a plethora of gems and sequins freshly purchased from Claire's Accessories and applied using his daughter's nail glue. The fake tan that he had applied was the colour of Pat's garden fence and was beginning to run in streaks down his face under the hot lights. He had clearly forgotten his 'Elvis shoes' and had therefore resorted to wearing his trainers that were meant to look designer but were clearly a cheap imitation. A cheap gold medallion hung around his neck and the black wig he was wearing made him look more Max Headroom than Elvis.

If the girls had been amused by his look, then they were totally hysterical once he started singing. Jude actually thought she was going to wet herself at his attempt at sexy gyrating. At one point, he came out into the audience to serenade members of the opposite sex, whilst curling his top lip and clumsily thrusting his groin in the general direction of the faces of the seated women. The words he was singing were completely unintelligible and he was permanently about a second behind his backing track. As he strutted back towards the stage, he attempted a mega-cool hop up the steps, tripped and almost face planted into the bloke on the sound desk.

"Fucking hell!" screamed Pat. "I've just pissed meself!"

Both teams had stopped playing to watch Brian from

Medway murder three of Elvis's finest, culminating in the worst rendition of American Trilogy that Jude had ever heard; at which point, Emma whipped her knickers off from under her skirt and lobbed them at the unfortunate Brian.

Jude was laughing so hard by this point that she almost couldn't breathe. Brian looked decidedly uncomfortable at this hitherto unheard-of occurrence and struggled to remove Emma's large comfy knickers from where they had landed across his shoulder. He then began to awkwardly wave them, like some kind of giant flag of surrender, whilst singing, 'Glory, glory, hallelujah, His truth is marching on!"

Unsurprisingly, the darts match had now taken a back seat by comparison and the girls continued to play distractedly as a succession of Elvis wannabes graced the small stage – each less convincing than the last.

Jude was amazed to discover that the labour club girls had actually emerged victorious, although in all honesty nobody much cared. They were presented with a trophy at the end of the night made from the finest plastic, and it was decided that whoever was brave enough to display the tacky ornament on their mantlepiece for the next twelve months, could have free drinks for the rest of the evening. In the end, Blossom agreed to keep the trophy and proceeded to make sure she got her money's worth in pints of lager!

"What a laugh!" slurred Jude, as she and Pat attempted to make their way across the un-lit holiday park at the end of the evening.

Just as the caravan park budget was limited for fixtures and fittings, so was the budget for outdoor lighting it seemed. Pat and Jude clung onto each other as they stumbled, tripped and wove their way along the uneven paths. At one point, Pat tripped and ended up in a bush, her legs sticking out, laughing her head off. Jude tried unsuccessfully to drag her to her feet, whilst laughing hysterically and almost falling in to join her. It took several minutes to untangle Pat from the bush, and they fell through their caravan door, with Pat covered in leaves and twigs and looking like a poorly camouflaged Gherka!

The two women gave up trying to boil the kettle that clearly didn't work and collapsed into bed, giggling like a couple of teenagers. Before long, both of them were fast asleep, with Pat snoring gently.

When Jude awoke, her mouth was as dry as the bottom of a budgie's cage and her head was banging. They managed to heat some water in a pan on the cooker and made a cup of coffee using the small jar that Pat had the foresight to bring with her – it also helped them to swallow the paracetamol that they both were desperate for.

"What a top night," said Pat.

"Bloody brilliant," said Jude. "Just what we needed."

"Do you think we'll ever find Ruby?" asked Pat, suddenly serious.

"I do hope so," replied Jude. "We're not giving up; no way!"

"You're a good friend," said Pat in a moment of raw emotion.

"You too Pat; you too," replied Jude squeezing Pat's hand. "Now let's round up the others, I think the bus is coming at 10."

"They'll be a lot quieter on the way home," smiled Pat.

"I bloody hope so," said Jude, "my head's killing me!"

Chapter Twenty-Two: The Journey Home

It was a much quieter crowd that entered the bus for the journey home. Emma was enviously showing no signs of a hangover, unlike Blossom who looked like death warmed up! Sarah was very subdued, and Jude doubted that she'd be volunteering to be sharing with Blossom and Apryl again any time soon! Apparently, the two 'lovebirds' had continued to party way into the night, drinking at least a bottle of Scotch between them, followed by some pretty vocal love-making – poor Sarah looked as if she hadn't slept a wink!

The bus began to pull out of the car park. Jude looked out of the window, as a man dressed in dark clothing passed by. He was wearing a cap and a hoodie, with the hood pulled up over the top of his cap. He was dressed almost completely in black, a cocky swagger to his stride. Jude could barely see the outline of his profile and yet, there was something strikingly familiar about him. She turned to ask Pat if she recognised him, but by the time they had both turned back, he had gone.

"All that booze has fried your brain," said Pat as she struggled to look for a man who was no longer there.

"I think you're right," sighed Jude, "I'm too old for this shit!"

The journey home was halted three times for Blossom to exit the bus urgently – it seemed her stomach was struggling to accept the huge quantity of lager and whisky that she had poured into it! The rest of the girls, although quieter than they had been, had quite a giggle reminiscing about Elvis.

"I hope Steve doesn't ask me where my knickers are!" laughed Emma, "They were my sexy ones too!"

"Christ, you could have carried your shopping home in them!" said Pat. "I've seen smaller hammocks!"

Jude and Pat were the first to be dropped off this time and they waved at the minibus as it pulled out of Pat's road.

"You gonna be alright?" asked Pat, knowing that Jude had been having a particularly grim time at home lately.

"Yeah, I'm ok," said Jude. "He'll be in a foul mood for certain. He was well pissed off with me for going away. I don't care anymore really – I just want to get out of there. I'm just so tired of it all."

"Come and stay here," said Pat.

"I can't," said Jude. "You don't want my shit on your doorstep."

"It's no bother honestly – and you know I definitely wouldn't offer if I didn't want to! Besides, I could do with the company. Just till you find somewhere," said Pat.

Jude thought long and hard. It was a very tempting offer. She didn't exactly have any worldly possessions to worry about; she could literally turn up with the clothes on her back and some clean drawers in a bag. It would put an end to her misery that's for sure – like finally ripping the plaster off an old wound.

"I'll think about," said Jude, "And maybe you should too. Take some time… so you don't offer something that you'd really rather not. I might out-stay my welcome!"

"My offer stands," said Pat. "You've got a room here if you want it."

Jude hugged her friend; she was definitely going to consider her offer. It might just be the spring-board she needed in her life right now.

Chapter Twenty-Three: Little Dean

Little Dean was stressed to fuck. The impending responsibility of fatherhood had scared the shit out of him, but it had also made him think about the state his life was in. He knew that he was punching way above his weight with Chelsea, and he didn't want to lose her, but he also knew that she had a lot more sense than to put up with his gangster shit. The truth was, he had dug such a hole for himself that he genuinely had no idea how he was going to crawl his way out of it. All this crap with Tommy Murphy was weighing down on him like a two-tonne weight and the police were on his case to tell them what he knew. They didn't have any hard evidence to link him directly with the attack that had left some poor fucker in intensive care with half his jaw missing, or else they would have arrested him; but they knew he had intel.

As a matter of fact, Dean had merely been a bystander at the time of the assault but, if they started digging around too long and uncovered any of his previous dealings with Tommy Murphy, then they would happily use him as a scape goat to pin some of this crap onto; of that he was certain. The old Bill wanted his kind off the streets and banged up, where he couldn't cause any hassle and, if he was honest, Dean wasn't sure he blamed them.

Little Dean had avoided both his Mum and Chelsea; he didn't really know what to say to either of them. Dean harboured more than a little guilt at the way he had treated his Mum in the last few years. He knew she had sat up for many a night, crying and worrying about him, and he knew that she loved him. He also knew that his father was a useless wanker, but he had chosen to side with him in an effort to play the 'big man.' Dean had sofa-surfed for the past fortnight, partly to avoid the issue, and partly to try and come up with some kind of plan; he had achieved neither. His trial was next week and, with this current round of grief, his future was not exactly fucking orange! What was he thinking, burgling some poor old biddy? What a fucking Knob!

Unsure of what the hell to do next, little Dean had come home. His Dad had passed him in the hallway on his way in muttering something about; 'Your mother's out slutting it with her fucking tart's darts!' Little Dean had grunted in reply, feeling little respect for his useless father – with an example like that, no wonder he was a total fuck-up! He sat down in the lounge that he now saw for the absolute dump it was and felt a surge of pity for his poor Mum, who had never been taken care of properly her whole life. He resolved to be a better son – once he got out of jail that was!

Chapter Twenty-Four: Jude & Little Dean

Jude was so surprised to see little Dean sitting in the dark front room, that she almost jumped out of her skin, "Christ! You scared the bloody life out of me!"

Dean didn't say anything in return. He just observed her with what could only be described as an anxious look.

If Jude had been worried about her son before, she was now completely disquieted. He looked broken.

"Do you want a cuppa?" asked Jude softly, not sure what else to offer him.

Little Dean continued to stare ahead of him. Jude stood for a few moments more, trying to give him the time he obviously needed. When she could stand the tension no longer, she threw caution to the wind and went over to her broken boy and put her arms around him. To her surprise, he did not push her away as she had feared he might, but returned the hug, burying his face into her neck. Jude felt the wetness of his silent tears and held him there, unspeaking. They embraced for the longest they had done in at least ten years and Jude guiltily realised that she was relishing the closeness, despite the obvious distress behind it.

Finally, Dean pulled away from her and wiped his eyes on the sleeve of his sweatshirt, sniffing noisily. He looked embarrassed by his rare outburst of emotion and hung his head.

"It's ok," said Jude kindly. "Even tough-men cry sometimes!"

Little Dean smiled weakly at his Mum's attempt at humour.

"I've been such a dick Mum and I'm in so much trouble!"

"Let's walk the dog," said Jude, "…like we used to. Besides I don't want your father coming home and poking his fucking oar in!"

Little Dean laughed openly at this and got up to find Buddy's lead, who was really enjoying this recent bout of dog walking that seemed to have become the new favourite pastime of his owners!

Jude changed into her comfy trainers and threw on a jacket. "Let's go to the bottom wreck," said Jude perceptively, referring to the field that was downhill from the estate and much quieter than the main park that was used by dog walkers, truanting school kids and probably the majority of the yobbos with whom her son was now depressingly involved. Jude was pretty sure that Dean would not want to be seen out walking with his Mum and, also, it was quite incredible how quickly people 'overheard' things on this estate.

They did not speak throughout their entire journey down to the bottom wreck. Jude was reluctant to begin the conversation. She didn't want to appear too pushy and she wanted to give Dean the time to consider what he wanted to say.

"I saw you at the police station," said Dean, seemingly as nervous about beginning the conversation as Jude was. The statement was more of a question and Jude knew that he probably wondered why she had been there.

"Someone we know has gone missing," said Jude, not giving any further details. "Were you there about your trial?"

"Not really," said Dean. "I've got some information that they want, but I can't grass!"

"Information about what?" asked Jude. "You have to remember Dean that no-one in this world will cover your arse for you – except me that is. The people who you think are your friends wouldn't spit on you if you were on fire…if it will help you in the long run, then you have to do what's right for you."

She paused before adding, "I've met Chelsea."

Little Dean stopped in his tracks and turned to face his Mum. He shook his head before exclaiming; "Fuck's sake!"

"It's ok Dean. I mean it's not exactly ideal, I'll grant you that, but she seems a nice girl. You definitely aren't getting anywhere with your current band of fuckwits holding you back!"

Dean laughed. "I do really like her Mum, but what good am I going to be to a baby? I like her too much to drag her into this shit..."

"What shit, exactly?" asked Jude, sitting down on a park bench and patting the space beside her for Dean to join her.

She had read somewhere, that difficult conversations were often best held when the two people involved were sat side by side – sort of less confrontational – but what the fuck did she know?! Anyway, it was worth a try and she had an uneasy feeling that Dean was bottling up something that had the makings of a very difficult conversation indeed.

"The police think I was involved. Involved in something really fucking nasty," said Dean quietly.

Jude's stomach lurched as she wondered how 'nasty' this something was.

"You can tell me," she said, resting her hand gently on Deans leg, but without changing her gaze from straight ahead.

"He kicked the shit out of him Mum. I thought he was going to fucking shoot him. I swear, I didn't do nothing!"

"Who did?" asked Jude nervously.

Dean took a deep breath, "Tommy Murphy!"

At this point Jude thought she going to being physically sick. She could feel the beads of sweat begin to trickle down her back, despite the cold Autumn air. She removed her hand from Dean's leg and began to run her fingers through her hair in an almost manic fashion. Tommy fucking Murphy! If she never heard that name again it would be too soon. First Ruby, now Dean. Tommy Murphy was trouble; trouble seemed to follow him around like the bloody plague, and recently he seemed to be dragging everyone she loved along with him!

Jude wanted to speak, but the words wouldn't come. She was seriously terrified now. If her boy had got himself involved with Tommy Murphy, then he really was in the shit. She wanted to say something positive, but she could not think of a single positive thing to say. She wanted to know exactly *how* Dean was involved with Tommy, but she wasn't sure she was strong enough to take the answer. She breathed in deeply, allowing the cold, crisp air to fill her lungs – steadying the trembling that was surging through her body. She continued to breathe in and out; quelling the panic, slowing her racing heartbeat.

"I want to come off the gear Mum," continued Dean. "I don't want this shit no more – I don't want the grief."

"Then you have to help them," said Jude, her voice barely a whisper. "What do you know?"

"I've been doing a bit of dealing, nothing much really. The old Bill don't have any proof of that, but they know I was there."

"Where?" asked Jude.

Little Dean explained that he had been going to visit Tommy for a pick-up on the day that another of his lackies had turned up without the money he owed Tommy. Tommy had proceeded to kick the absolute shit out of this lad, who was barely a kid himself. The boy had been kicked, punched, stamped on and finally pistol-whipped with a gun supplied by another of Dean's friends. Dean had witnessed the entire attack but had played no part. It seemed that the police were not after Dean for his involvement in the incident, but more for the fact that they were sure that he knew where Tommy Murphy could be hiding. The young lad had ended up in intensive care and was now on life support in an induced coma, waiting for the swelling in his brain to go down before they could wake him up – that's if he ever woke up.

The police were desperate to bag Tommy Murphy once and for all and, if it meant putting the screws on lads like

Dean Junior, then they were fully prepared to do it. The last thing Dean needed was for them to go poking further into his business and discover his prior involvement with Tommy Murphy. If they had any evidence of his drug dealing – whether it be small time or not – then Dean would be going to prison for quite some time. On top of his burglary charge, he was fucked!

"They want me to tell him where he is Mum," said Dean hopelessly.

"And do you know where he is," asked Jude, her nerves calming as anger took their place. Tommy Murphy needed locking up once and for all. She didn't dare imagine what state Ruby was in right now and her fears for her safety magnified ten-fold.

"I can't grass on him Mum, they'll fucking kill me!" said Dean.

"You can grass on him and you will," said Jude, surprised at the forcefulness of her tone. "Tommy Murphy is *not* God-all-fucking-Mighty, and he needs sorting out! If that boy dies, this will be murder and you do *not* want to be implicated in any way!"

Dean shook his head with the desperation of a condemned man.

"Dean! Look at me!" said Jude, all thoughts of a non-confrontational conversation leaving her head. "If you tell them where he is, it could really help your trial – show you want to reform. Besides; it's not just you that you have to think of now. Whether you want to be with Chelsea or not, you are that baby's father, and that baby will come whether you are ready or not – don't let the poor little bugger grow up with a waste-of-space for a father; you're better than that!" Jude could have added "...like your father..." at this point but she didn't; although the way little Dean looked at her, she knew he understood completely.

Dean nodded his head just a fraction. He knew his Mum was right. He also knew that if he didn't co-operate with the police, and Tommy somehow dragged him deeper into this mess, his life would be over anyway. Basically, he could remain loyal to a load of idiots who wouldn't piss on him if he was on fire and spend the next 20 years doing bird for someone else's fuck-up, or he could man-up and 'cover his own arse,' as his Mum had rightly put it!

"Where is he?" asked Jude.

"He's in a caravan…" began Dean.

"…in fucking Minster!" exclaimed Jude, finishing Dean's sentence.

"How the fuck do you know *that*?" asked Dean, incredulously.

"Never mind how I know that," said Jude, her mind racing back to the figure in the hoodie that she had seen on their Tart's Darts trip to the holiday park. She *knew* she'd recognised Tommy's arrogant swagger, the moment she had glimpsed him through the minibus window!

"You need to get yourself down that police station and tell them exactly what you know, but I want you to wait until I say," said Jude. She was unsure what the hell she was going to do, but she knew she had to get hold of Pat immediately.

"Mum, you're scaring me," said Dean, hardly recognising the force to be reckoned with that his mother seemed to have become overnight!

"I'll be fine," said Jude, having little faith in her own words. "He's got a young girl and a baby with him and that fucker better not harm one hair on their heads! He needs locking up Dean!"

"Mum, shouldn't you let the police deal with it?" said Dean, hardly believing that he was giving his own mother advice on how to follow the law!

"If he gets wind that they're on to him, he'll hurt her just to shut her up. It wouldn't surprise me if he took her and the baby hostage as insurance!" said Jude, now more certain than ever that she and Pat had to get Ruby out of there. "Do you know anything about his movements?"

"Not really," said Dean, "although he does have a regular meet on a Thursday night – but don't ask me where 'cos I ain't telling you!"

"I don't need to know *where* that bastard goes to, I just need to know *when*," replied Jude. Ruby had often wondered why Tommy made so little protest about her Thursday night Darts nights and had shared this thought with Pat and Jude. It was beginning to become clear that Tommy obviously did something big on a Thursday and was more than happy for Ruby to be out of the way.

"Right, today is Wednesday," said Jude. "You need to lay low until I get back, then get yourself straight up to that police station. If you don't tell them now, you'll land me and at least three other people in deep shit!"

"Fucking hell Mum!" said Dean at a loss for words. "What are you gonna do?"

"The less you know the better," smiled Jude, "Just make sure you do the right thing!"

"Shall I go home?" asked Dean, wondering where he should stay until Friday.

"No, you don't want to risk your Dad finding out, else he'll put his two penneth in and fuck everything up," said Jude. "…Besides you don't want any of your cronies sniffing round you either. I know exactly where you can go, but any drugs and I'll bloody string you up myself!"

Chapter Twenty-Five: Pat & Jude

As soon as Jude had got back from the bottom wreck, she had gone straight round to Pat's house, dragging a bewildered Dean behind her. She had more or less made him wear a disguise, and she herself was dressed entirely in black and wearing a hood pulled up over her head – something which she absolutely never did.

Pat had opened the door before Jude had time to ring the doorbell, having seen the unlikely looking duo rushing up her path, heads down, like a couple of secret agents!

Jude had taken barely minutes to fill Pat in on recent developments. Little Dean had sat on Pat's sofa in the front room feeling decidedly nervous about whatever plan his Mum, and some old looking bird who looked a bit like Peggy Mitchell, were discussing in hushed voices in the kitchen.

Jude had explained that she now knew where Tommy Murphy was hiding and that she knew he was likely to be out tomorrow night. She had apologetically asked if Little Dean could stay at Pat's whilst he waited for the right time to visit the Police station.

Being the loyal friend that Pat was, she had agreed to little Dean laying low whilst her and Jude went to the holiday camp, under the cover of darkness, to try and rescue Ruby. The two women were certain that was where she would be, and they were also aware of the very real danger they were potentially putting themselves into. However, they both knew that they had to at least try to get Ruby out of there before the Police swooped – if Ruby was in that caravan when they bashed the door in, Pat and Jude were convinced that Tommy Murphy would kill her rather than let her go.

That evening, the unlikely trio sat in Pat's sitting room, eating a Chinese and watching the TV without paying any real heed to what was being said. There was very little conversation between them – each deep in their own thoughts – each very afraid of what their future held in store.

Pat had made a comment about her and Jude being Bunkers Hill's answer to 'Hart to Hart,' to which Dean had jokily replied, "More like Tart to Tart!"

The laughter they had shared at this point, had gone some way to relieving the tension in the room and Jude thought she caught the tiniest glimpse of the boy she loved, returning to his former self. She hoped with all her heart that he would find his way out of the mess he was in and make a better life for himself. Her voice had choked with emotion when she had told him that she would support both him and Chelsea when the baby came – no matter where he might be at that time. The thought of her son spending time behind bars was one that she dreaded becoming a reality, but she knew she had to remain strong for all of them.

Jude had also told little Dean that her marriage to his father was over and that she intended to leave him once this recent situation was resolved. Dean Junior had not been at all surprised by her revelation and, if he felt any emotion at all, he certainly didn't show it. Dean Senior had given up calling Jude's mobile over the past week, having received no response from his errant wife. Jude really did not have the energy to talk about things – let alone row about it – there really was nothing more to be said. In honesty, any distress that Dean Senior may have harboured about the impending departure of his wife, would be solely due to his desire to 'save face' rather than any kind of heart break. Jude doubted he would even notice that she had gone; until he ran out of clean pants that was.

Pat and Jude had booked a taxi for early in the morning with Tony, who had been a mate of Alf's. Tony had agreed to prioritise any calls from them during the day and had agreed to be solely at their disposal during the whole of Thursday evening, for a very reasonable fee. He had not asked for any explanation regarding their unusual booking requirements and Pat had thanked for his ability to, "keep his nose out!" Alf had been very well liked by many, and those that remained loyal to him, also remained loyal to Pat.

When they had retired to bed for the evening, Pat had warned Little Dean that if he bought any drugs into her house she would, "Chop his fucking bollocks off and make him wear them as earrings!" Little Dean had laughed, but there was a nervousness in his laughter that showed that he knew she meant what she said!

Jude said nothing more to Dean about why she and Pat were going to the holiday park. He didn't know Ruby, except by name, and Jude knew that the less he knew, the better for both him and Ruby. They had agreed a simple code between them – Jude would send a text when it was time for Dean to go to the Police station and she had made him swear that he would go the moment he received the text; no matter what the time. This would mean that by some miracle, Pat and Jude had managed to rescue Ruby and Jude wanted the police hot on Tommy's tail before he came looking for them. If the text message read, 'Please come home x,' then Dean was to go to the station and tell the Police everything he knew about Tommy Murphy; his whereabouts, his attack on the young lad, and the threats that he had also made to Little Dean. (Little Dean had reluctantly shared this with Jude when she had further questioned his reluctance to co-operate; basically, he was absolutely shitting himself!)

However, if the text message read, 'Where are you?' he was to bolt all the doors, phone the Police and tell them that his Mum and Pat were in grave danger. This message would mean that Tommy had somehow rumbled Pat and Jude's attempt to free Ruby and he had wreaked the kind of revenge that only a Murphy was capable of. This scenario was one that Jude did not want to dwell on for too long – the outcome did not bear thinking about.

Both of the agreed text messages were ones that Jude regularly sent to her son, and therefore would raise no suspicions if the Police confiscated Dean's phone for any reason. It would also mean that little Dean was in no way implicated in Jude's plans, nor could he be labelled a grass; when, and if, Tommy Murphy got caught. The word on the street would simply be that Dean had visited the Police in connection with the burglary he had committed. Jude was not naïve enough to realise that Dean's life could be made very difficult if the truth came out - both with his 'mates' and, God forbid, if Tommy managed to escape capture for some reason.

Chapter Twenty-Six: The Holiday Park

Pat and Jude had set off early as they wanted to get to the park before anyone was up and about – they guessed that if Tommy conducted most of his 'business' in the dark, then he wasn't likely to up with the lark the next day. They wanted to use the time to have a snoop around the park to see if they could find out which caravan the runaways were in.

It was not a particularly large site, although Jude had no idea how they were going to find the exact van. Fortunately, Jude did not think Tommy knew her and Pat well enough to recognise them from a distance; although she and Pat had taken no chances. They had dressed in dark and non-descript clothing, neither of them was wearing make-up, and both had on sunglasses and a wig that Pat had dug out of her 'fancy dress' box. Pat loved any excuse to dress up and had a startling assortment of wigs and costume clobber. If the situation hadn't been so serious then Jude would have wet herself laughing at the sight of her and Pat looking like a pair of badly dressed transvestites!

"Fuck's sake!" exclaimed Pat as she caught sight of herself in the taxi's rear-view mirror.

"Going somewhere special ladies?" smirked a bemused Tony.

"You say one bloody word..." warned Pat.

Jude couldn't help but laugh out loud at this point. If any of the Labour Club girls could see them now, they'd think they'd lost their sodding marbles!

"I hope that girl appreciates this," said Pat. "I ain't gone out without make-up in twenty years!"

"I think make-up is the least of your worries," laughed Jude.

"Speak for yourself!" said Pat in mock temper.

Once they had managed to quell their hysteria, Pat and Jude descended into a nervous silence for the rest of the journey. They may have looked ridiculous, but what they were about to attempt was not funny in the slightest.

The taxi pulled up in the small holiday site carpark. Pat handed him a piece of paper with both her and Jude's phone numbers written on it – "If you don't hear from us by midnight, then we may be in trouble."

"You ain't doing nothing too stupid are you? Your Alf will come and bloody haunt me if you get yourself hurt," said Tony, his voice thick with concern.

"We'll be fine," said Pat, although Jude was feeling less confident by the second.

Tony left the carpark reluctantly, after assurances from Pat that he had nothing to worry about – unless they didn't call him, that was!

Once the taxi had disappeared into the distance, Jude turned to Pat and asked, "Ok Cagney, what the fuck do we do now?!"

"This was your sodding idea!" said Pat.

Jude sighed in agreement – she couldn't deny the fact that this had indeed been her idea, although Pat had willingly come along for this crazy ride.

"We'll be fine," said Jude, finding a little confidence from deep within her. "I suggest we spend the day sort of wandering around, but laying low, if you know what I mean? We'll keep in the background, but keep our eyes peeled; if you see a caravan door opening anywhere, then we need to get there pronto and see who leaves or enters."

For the rest of the morning, the two friends did just that. They must have circled the site at least twenty or thirty times, keeping out of sight, hiding behind bushes like cartoon characters in a Bugs Bunny movie. They visited the small play area, in case Ruby had perhaps taken Reuben for a little breath of fresh air, but there was no sign of any of them. Fortunately, the site was really quiet as it was not peak season and so, there were several caravans that were clearly unoccupied, or shut down for the winter, which meant there were less places to try and watch. After several hours of creeping around and loitering in dark corners, Pat had finally had enough.

"It's no good Jude," she said. "My feet are bloody killing me, and my back's hurting from crouching over like the bleeding hunch back of Notre Dame. I need a cup of tea."

"Me too," said Jude, beginning to wonder what the bloody hell they were hoping to find. Silly old fools; thinking they could spring Ruby from her nutty boyfriend, just by wearing a couple of stupid wigs and hiding in bushes on a deserted holiday park.

"We won't give up though," said Pat, squeezing Jude's arm as she sensed her friend's despair. "Just a quick cuppa, and maybe a bacon buttie, and then we'll go back to sitting in cold, wet bushes!" she smiled. As she said this, Jude thought she couldn't have loved a friend more – the woman was a diamond.

They went through to the grubby-looking café directly opposite the small supermarket that sold overpriced tiny boxes of washing powder, kid's fishing nets and other totally random 'essentials.' The bored looking waitress came over to their table and took their order, with all the grace of one who was doing them a giant favour.

"Fuck me, do you reckon the charm school was shut?" asked Pat, none-too-quietly once the waitress had begun to walk away.

Jude did not answer. She had stopped dead in her tracks and was staring directly at the shop across the road.

"What?" asked Pat, noticing Jude's pre-occupation.

"Sssssh!" said Jude, slinking down in her chair, whilst never taking her eyes from the shop doorway.

Pat followed her friend's gaze, "Jesus Christ!" she exclaimed, in a hushed voice.

The two women rose from their chairs in unison, just as the waitress returned to their table, carrying a teapot and two mugs.

Pat thrust a ten-pound note into the girl's apron pocket, "We'll have it later," she said, as she and Jude rushed towards the café door.

The girl gave an exasperated sigh and stomped back in the direction of the counter. Pat and Jude paused at the café entrance, making sure that the outlines of the figures that they had both instantly recognised were safely inside the shop before they fully exited the café. There was a large bin store to the left of the building, and Pat and Jude eased themselves behind it, never once taking their eyes from the little supermarket.

There was no mistaking the arrogant swagger of Tommy Murphy dressed, as usual, in his trademark joggers that hung halfway down his arse, and a hoodie pulled up over a peaked cap depicting allegiance to some New York Crew or another. Jude thought that ironically, she and Pat were dressed in almost identical attire!

Tommy's companion however, caused Jude's heart to sink into the pit of her stomach. There was no doubt that it was Ruby, if only by the fact that she pushing a tatty looking buggy carrying a sleeping Reuben, but what was most horrifying was the state of her general appearance. She had never been a big girl, but she was now barely skin and bone; her skinny jeans hung off a body that did not possess enough fat to fill them. The dark curls that she had once proudly tended, hung in greasy strings down her back and she shuffled with the gait of someone who had lost every ounce of fight in them. From their hiding place, it was not possible to see if she was injured, but the way she was shuffling, like a frail old lady, was truly upsetting.

Pat and Jude exchanged a look that spoke volumes; they were now more certain than ever that they had to get her out of there.

Chapter Twenty-Seven: The Caravan

Pat's heart was now beating so violently in her chest, she felt sure it could be heard out loud. Her palms were clammy, and she no longer felt the coldness of the damp, Autumn air. That fucker! By the state of Ruby, she wondered how much longer the poor girl would have lasted, locked up here with the lunatic bastard that was Tommy Murphy. An overwhelming sense of anger began to overtake the fear that had threatened to undermine her courage – she be damned if she'd be running scared any time soon.

The supermarket doors slid open, and Tommy and Ruby appeared in the entrance. Reuben had awoken from his nap and was now crying. Jude's heart bled, as Ruby tried ineffectively to calm the anxious tot. Tommy pushed her none-too-gently from behind, urging her forward.

"Wanker!" exclaimed Pat, under her breath.

"Ssssh!" whispered Jude. "We'll have to try and follow them, but for Christ's sake, don't let them see you!"

Jude knew that if Tommy, or Ruby for that matter, caught one glimpse of her and Pat, then the shit was really going to hit the fan. Jude was sure that Ruby wanted to leave, but she really did not have faith in the young girl's current state of mind – she doubted Ruby had an ounce of strength or courage left in her. If Ruby saw them now, Jude worried that it would put the fear of God into her. She certainly wouldn't feel reassured by Pat and Jude's presence – quite the opposite in fact.

Pat and Jude stayed in their hiding place for several seconds as they carefully watched Tommy, Ruby and Reuben walk up the path towards the first row of vans. As soon as their targets turned left, Pat and Jude crept from behind the bin store and into a patch of undergrowth that gave them a clearer view. Fortunately, they were able to catch a glimpse as Tommy and Ruby lifted the buggy up the steps of a caravan that was only about halfway up the row. Once they were sure that the door had closed, they both let out an enormous sigh of relief. Up until that point, Jude did not realise that she had actually been holding her breath; and it seemed that Pat had been doing the very same thing!

"Now what?" asked Jude.

"Now we just sit it out until he leaves," whispered Pat.

"That could be fucking hours!" exclaimed Jude. "If he leaves at all."

"He'll leave," said Pat. "We've just got to be patient. Now I think we're gonna be here for quite some time, so I suggest we get prepared. You go and get something for us to eat and drink and I'll keep watch, but for fuck's sake, keep your phone on!"

Jude left Pat, who was making her way a little further up the path into a less conspicuous spot, and one which afforded her a clearer view of the caravan. She hurried across the path in the direction of the café. She felt the need to continuously look over her shoulder, in case she was being followed, and she was jumpier than a cat on a hot tin roof. How criminals lived like this all the time, beggared belief – a few hours of being on high alert and her nerves were shot to bits.

Jude entered the café, to be met by the petulant young waitress, who stared at her, arms folded, like a disgruntled parent waiting for their child to come home.

"Can I take those bacon butties now please?" asked Jude. In different circumstances, she would have reminded the stroppy girl that, as the customer, she was supposed to be treated with a bit more respect, but the last thing Jude wanted right now was to draw any kind of attention to herself.

"Can I also have the teas to take away please?" said Jude.

The girl huffed, "Well you'll to wait now cos I'll have to re-make them."

"That's fine," said Jude, giving her best 'fake-smile.'

Jude stood at the counter whilst the girl, whose name badge identified her as Celeste, banged and crashed her way through the obviously arduous task of putting a couple of tea bags into two paper cups. Celeste then began to deliver Jude's order one item at a time; first one cup of tea, then the lid. Then the next cup of tea, then the lid. Then one bacon roll…and so on. Jude tried not to look impatient, God forbid, she should rattle the girl and slow up proceedings – any slower and she'd be ordering her sodding Christmas lunch! Jude thought that the name Celeste was quite appropriate, like the Mary Celeste; vacant!

Eventually when a grand total of four items had been dumped unceremoniously on the counter in front of Jude, and Jude had managed to help Celeste calculate the total amount owed when two Kit Kats were added to an order that had already been partly paid for, Jude finally left the café. She wasn't sure how much more stress she could take and, if they got out of this unscathed, she was going to binge drink the biggest bottle of Bacardi she could manage!

"Bloody hell, I thought you'd got lost," said Pat, when Jude finally returned.

Pat had managed to find a recess between two caravans almost directly opposite where Tommy and Ruby were staying. An assortment of garden furniture and discarded toys provided the perfect screen for them to hide behind, as well as a place to park their bottoms. It wasn't the most comfortable seating arrangement, but Jude was just grateful to be out of view. They ate the bacon rolls greedily, despite them being barely luke-warm. Neither of them had eaten since breakfast, and both were starving. The tea and Kit Kats went down a treat.

Pat looked at her watch, "2 o'clock, let's hope he goes out early today."

The two women sat huddled together for the next four hours. Jude had now lost all feeling in her toes and she was stiff from perching on the edge of a wonky garden table. Poor old Pat, who could have given Jude at least 20 years, must have been really suffering; although she hadn't moaned a bit – she was a tough old bird for sure.

The daylight had almost entirely faded, and it was really quite dark. The lights had been on in the caravan for a couple of hours now, and Jude was grateful that they were able to use them as an indication of occupation.

"Look," said Pat in hushed tones, grabbing Jude's arm as she tried to change into a comfier position on the table.

Jude followed Pat's pointed finger with her eyes. As she squinted, she could just make out Tommy Murphy's outline emerging through the narrow caravan doorway. Pat and Jude both crouched down as far as they could go in their hiding place.

"Text Tony," whispered Pat. "We need him to be waiting in the car park for us. I don't wanna be stranded out here with a broken girl and a baby, waiting to be caught by Tommy Murphy!"

Jude shielded the light on her phone as she sent a quick message to Tony. He replied almost immediately – bless him – he was clearly worried about them both.

Pat and Jude both held their breath as Tommy walked past their hiding place; they could hear him talking on the phone, using words like' bruv' and 'innit.' Jude held onto her breath so deeply she thought her lungs would burst; she was terrified that he would hear them. After what seemed like an eternity, Pat and Jude watched Tommy Murphy's black outline disappear in the direction of the car park. Shortly after, there was a screech of tyres as Tommy's ride left the site.

"Fuck me!" exclaimed Jude. "I think I've just wet myself!"

Pat gave a quiet laugh, "You'll have to cross your legs for a bit longer duck, we've got to get in and out of that van right away."

The two friends crept out of the shadows and up the path towards their unsuspecting friend. Jude hoped that Ruby wouldn't be too frightened to leave – she was quite prepared to drag her kicking and screaming if necessary!

Pat and Jude approached the caravan with caution, listening for the sound of voices; they both hoped that none of Tommy's cronies were left inside. Jude pressed her ear to the caravan door but could hear nothing except the faint crying of a baby. A lump caught in her throat as she imagined how miserable that poor baby must have been these past few weeks.

Pat climbed the steps and eased the door open – nothing could have prepared her or Jude for the carnage that lay before them. The cramped space stank of stale food and decay. There was the unmistakeable stench of weed that clung to the worn fabric of every cushion and curtain in the place. Ashtrays over-flowed on every available surface and empty beer bottles and crisp packets littered the floor.

Reuben's cries could be heard in what must have been one of the bedrooms. He made the sound of a baby who had literally cried himself dry, deep sobs, interspersed by large, staccato intakes of breath that fell on deaf ears. Jude felt like sobbing herself. The scene was so utterly depressing, so terrifyingly hopeless that it shook her to her core.

"Oh my fucking Christ!" shrieked Pat, rousing Jude from her stunned silence.

Jude had not seen Ruby, although Pat clearly had. She was lying on the sofa and it looked like she was barely conscious. Her pale, limp form was draped across the sofa, one leg trailing down towards the floor, her body seemingly lifeless.

Pat rushed across the room and put her ear to Ruby's mouth and nose.

"She's still breathing," she said; the relief evident in her voice.

"We have to get them out of here," said Jude going to

the bedroom to retrieve the now hysterical Reuben. She cradled his sweaty body into her bosom, stroking his dark curls as she tried to soothe him. She kissed the top of his head, over and over again, her heart breaking at his distress. His nappy was full and damp, and he smelled of stale milk and neglect.

Pat took her phone from her pocket and dialled Tony's number, "Hi Tony I need you to come to us. There isn't time to explain but just get your car as near to van number 27 as you can – and please hurry up!"

Within seconds, Jude heard a car engine outside. She threw open the door, now oblivious to the whereabouts of Tommy – she just wanted these kids out of danger.

Between the three of them, they managed to carry Ruby to the car, she barely stirred as they lifted her, and Jude prayed that they were not too late to save her.

Jude sent a quick text to Little Dean, "When you coming home? X" as agreed. The rest of the journey she cradled Reuben tight as Tony drove the three of them to the hospital. Tony said nothing on their journey.

Chapter Twenty-Eight: Little Dean

Little Dean almost jumped on top of the coffee table as his phone pinged. He read the text – his heart pounding in his chest. He fucking hoped Tommy hadn't hurt his Mum, and that daft friend of hers.

His relief at the message was quickly followed by the stark realisation that he was about to grass on Tommy Murphy. If he was honest with himself, he would probably have backed out of the deal if he could, but now that his Mum and Pat had obviously been successful in whatever hair brained scheme they had hatched between them, it wouldn't be long before Tommy Murphy was on the war path – and guess who he'd be making a beeline for?!

Little Dean pulled his hoodie up over his head. He left Pat's house via the back gate; he didn't want any prying eyes looking into his business. He lit a cigarette and drew in a deep lungful of smoke. He walked with his head down, checking behind him as he went.

He wondered what Chelsea was doing tonight. He hoped that he wouldn't be away too long. In happier circumstances he would have enjoyed being in a proper home like Pat's. A home where the sheets smelled of washing powder, where the kettle was always on, and you didn't have the threat of the Old Bill bashing on your front door. The places where he had stayed over the past few months, years even, had never been anything like a home. He realised that he longed to feel at home again. He wanted Chelsea, and he wanted his baby – he didn't want the shitty life he had made for himself anymore.

Little Dean arrived at the Police station – no matter how 'straight' he became, he knew he would never feel comfortable in these places. He spoke to the desk sergeant, giving his name.

"Dean Jackson…I've come to give you what you need," he sighed.

It was mere moments before Little Dean was ushered into one of the interview rooms. There, he told the officer where he believed Tommy was hiding. He told him about the attack and the threats he had received himself. He neglected to mention about the drug runs that he had done for Tommy – but then they didn't need to know everything!

The officer wrote at length, listening carefully to Dean's statement. He only spoke to ask for clarification or for specific details. Unbelievably, Little Dean was relieved when the officer suggested that he remain in the cell overnight, for his own protection as much as anything. When asked if he felt his life was in danger from Tommy Murphy, Little Dean had replied truthfully that he was certain it was.

The officer thanked him for his time and led him through to one of the cells, leaving Dean with a blanket, a cup of tea and a cheese sandwich. If the truth be told, Little Dean felt safer in a cell than he would have done, hiding at Pat's house, with Tommy fucking Murphy running around like a rabid dog!

Chapter Twenty-Nine: Tommy Murphy

It was long after midnight when Tommy returned back to the van. He was buzzing and desperately needed a comedown. He had a large bag of some rather potent skunk in his pocket and he was looking forward to a smoke.

He noticed the partially open door immediately. With the filth on his tail, he was hyper alert to every change. He didn't for one minute, think that Ruby wouldn't be where he left her – passed out on the couch. At least he couldn't hear the brat screaming anymore – fucking kid!

He pushed the door further open. He peered into the room. Everything was exactly as it had been. Everything except for the empty space where Ruby had been, that was.

"Fucking bitch!" he screamed.

Tommy began charging through the caravan like a rampaging bull – he slung open every door and cupboard; uncertain of what he expected to find. All he knew for sure was that the bitch had disappeared, and she knew far too fucking much for his liking.

"Bitch!" he yelled. He was, by now, almost manic and had started to pace up and down the length of the small van, banging his fists into the walls. How dare she? How fucking *dare* she leave him? As he paced, he attempted to control the fiery pit of anger that bubbled in the pit of his stomach, threatening to spew out like an erupting volcano. In his wired and paranoid state, he began to imagine all manner of conspiracies that may have led to Ruby's departure but then; how the fuck *had* she managed to leave him? The Valium that he had been dropping into her tea these past few weeks in attempt to keep her subdued was pretty strong, and the dose he had given her this evening had knocked her out completely. In fact, at one point, he had almost feared that he might had given her an overdose; so how the fuck had she managed to get out of the van? She certainly was in no fit state to walk out; which meant only one thing…*someone* had carried her out!

At the realisation that Ruby had most likely managed to involve a third party to help her, Tommy's rage bubbled over. By the time he was spent, the caravan was completely trashed. All he needed to do now was find that bitch and keep her gob shut once and for all!

Tommy went back into the small kitchen area and retrieved the gun that was hidden behind the pipe at the back of the sink. One thing he didn't need was the Gavvers finding that little gem if they finally tracked him down – he needed to dispose of it for good really, but he quite liked the Kudos it gave him.

He shoved the gun down the back of his trousers and went towards the door…

"Put your arms above your head!" came the command. "Put your arms above your head and stay still!"

Tommy made a run for the door, but he was bundled to the floor by three large, muscular bodies.

"Get the fuck off me you bastards!" he yelled, scratching and biting like a scalded alley cat.

The officers fought to cuff him, but Tommy was not giving up without a fight. He reached for an empty beer bottle which he cracked across the nearest head, whilst tightening his grip on the bunch of hair that he was trying to wrench from its roots. Tommy felt the unmistakeable sting of the pepper spray as it burned into his eyes. He screamed out in pain, releasing his grip on his assailant's hair. Within in an instant, his arms were wrenched behind his back and cuffed tightly. Tommy continued to kick and bite until his legs too were bound up behind his back.

"You're nicked son," panted the triumphant officer, blood running in a scarlet trail down his forehead and cheeks.

Tommy spat and screamed in frustration. The pepper spray was searing into his face and he could barely see through the tears that were now pouring from his eyes.

After patting him down roughly, the officers retrieved

the gun from his waistband and a good-sized bag of gear from his jacket pocket – Tommy Murphy was in deep shit now! With the forensics they would undoubtedly get from the gun, as well as the charge of attempted murder on the boy still clinging to life in intensive care, Tommy was going to be at her Majesty's Pleasure for the foreseeable. Add to that the charge of resisting arrest and assaulting an officer, as well as the stash of weed in his pocket; it was a done deal as they say.

Tommy Murphy was bundled into the back of a meat wagon yelling, "CUNTS!" at the top of his voice.

Chapter Thirty: Little Dean

Dean lay in his cell listening to the carnage that was taking place in the main reception area of the Police Station. Without a doubt he recognised that voice and the venom spilling from its owner. He pulled the rough, prison-style blanket up over his ears and kept his gob well and truly shut – there was no fucking way he wanted Tommy Murphy to know he was here. The only good thing was, that when Tommy found out, as he undoubtedly would, that Little Dean had been in the nick that night, he would think he couldn't possibly have been connected to any of the night's happenings. Dean only hoped his Mum was still ok, he didn't dare imagine what mess she had got herself in to.

At around five o'clock the next morning, Dean was awoken by the unmistakeable clank of his cell door opening, and he thought, depressingly, that it would be a sound he was about to become used to after his impending trial next week.

The desk sergeant checked him out and thanked him for his co-operation. Dean replied with a wry smile and a shrug of his shoulders; he hoped that all this shit would be worth it in the end when he stood before the judge.

Once he was out of the Police station, Dean was at a bit of a loss as to what his next move should be. He wanted to avoid the boys on the estate like the Plague, and he hadn't a clue where his Mum and Pat were. He was worried about sending a text – it was something he hadn't done in the longest time he realised guiltily – but also, he didn't want to get her into trouble if she was fuck knows where, with fuck knows who! In the end, he could bear the suspense no longer and sent a quick message that simply read, "Wher u at?"

Chapter Thirty One: Ruby

Ruby opened her eyes slowly, the light was blinding, and her head was banging like a drum. It took several moments for her to become accustomed to her surroundings and she slowly realised that she was lying in a hospital bed.

"Reuben?" she called frantically, struggling to sit up, before crashing back down onto the pillows as her frail body gave way.

"It's ok," said Pat, reaching across from the chair in which she had been dozing at the side of Ruby's bed.

"Pat?" asked Ruby. "What happened? Reuben...is he....," her voice cracked with emotion.

"Reuben is fine," said Pat, stroking Ruby's arm. "Auntie Jude's taken him for a drink; bloody woman's so broody I'm scared she's gonna lay a sodding egg!"

Ruby smiled, the effort of trying to speak taking every ounce of energy she possessed.

"You gave us quite a scare," said Pat. She hadn't said anything to Jude, but she had been so scared that Ruby was going to die, and the level of emotion she had felt had scared her even more. "That fucking bastard...."

"Is he? Is Tommy here?" asked Ruby, suddenly terrified.

"That shit bag ain't going nowhere for the foreseeable," said Pat, a wave of anger coursing through her veins. "Me and Jude got you out of there like James fucking Bond!"

Ruby managed a weak laugh. "Oh my God, what did you do?"

Pat began to tell Ruby of how she and Jude had dressed up like the Milk Tray Man – completely in black – with a couple of dodgy wigs and some even dodgier shades; before embarking on their very own stake out, armed only with a cold bacon butty and a mobile phone.

"Bloody hell," said Ruby, "You could have got yourselves killed!"

"It was worth it," said Pat. "But I swear if you ever go back to that bastard, I'll string you up meself!"

"It's done now," said Ruby, feeling suddenly tearful.

"Now, now, stop your blubbering," said Pat. "You just concentrate on getting yourself better, he'd filled you full of Valium you know…and you don't look like you've washed or eaten in weeks."

"Oh Pat," cried Ruby, "It was awful, I was so scared." And then the tears fell in earnest.

When Jude re-entered Ruby's hospital room, she saw that Pat was holding Ruby tightly, whilst sobs wracked the defeated girl's body. Reuben wriggled in her arms, he was a happier chap now he had been cuddled and fed; the remnants of several chocolate cookies still visible on his chubby, pink cheeks.

At the sight of his Mum, he began to babble and coo, calling, "mum, mum, mum."

Ruby pulled away from Pat's arms and smiled at her boy. The guilt she felt for almost failing him so badly was indescribable, but she vowed to herself, in that moment, to never let another man come between them in the way Tommy had.

Jude placed Reuben carefully on the bed so that Ruby could touch his face – the bond between them was still so strong and Jude thanked God they had found them both in time.

It wasn't long before Ruby was exhausted; the toll of the last few weeks beginning to show.

Pat was the first to speak; "Listen girl, we're going to go home; we are all shattered. The doctors say you'll be out of here by tomorrow, so we'll come back in the morning."

"But what about Reuben…" asked Ruby.

"He will be just fine with Auntie Jude," laughed Pat, "If she ever lets the poor little bugger go that is! We'll be back tomorrow and when we come to collect you, you're coming home to stay with me – just till you get yourself sorted…no matter how long it takes."

"But I can't," said Ruby, not wishing to impose.

"You can, and you bloody well will," said Pat kindly. "It ain't like you've got much choice anyway is it? Now don't you dare argue with me my girl, I won't listen anyway!"

"She's right there," laughed Jude, "she doesn't do much listening once her mind is made up. Now get plenty of sleep and we'll be back in the morning. Your boy will be well cared for, Tommy is safely in a cage where he belongs, and you've got a safe place to come home to once you're out."

"You didn't have to do this," said Ruby softly.

"No, we didn't," said Jude, "But I can't remember the last time I got to sit in a bush for 6 hours, wearing a dodgy wig and a pair of soggy knickers!"

"Euggh! Don't ask!" laughed Pat. "Now SLEEP! And we'll see you tomorrow."

As the two women left, Ruby began to cry again, but this time the emotion she felt was one of pure gratitude; no-one had treated her with such kindness in her whole life and she didn't have the faintest idea how she could ever repay them for that.

Chapter Thirty-Two: Back at the Club

The Labour Club girls were back together again. Jude couldn't remember when she'd ever felt so contented. Sure, there had been some real strife over the past eight months, and Jude knew there would likely be more to follow, but things were rosier than they had ever been.

Thursday darts nights had continued with full force and the rest of the girls were more than a little in awe of the bravery that Pat and Jude had shown. They were pleased to have Ruby back with them; and in one piece thankfully.

"What you drinking?" called Pat from her position at the bar. "Usual?"

"Yep, same as," called Jude.

Ruby sat on Jude's left, barely recognisable from the shell of a girl she and Pat had rescued all those months ago. She had put on quite a few pounds, weight which she had desperately needed. Her hair had regained its former glossy shine, and her curls hung down her back in beautiful ringlets as they had done before 'Tommy-gate.' No longer was her face scarred by the tell-tale signs of an undeserved beating and no more did she flinch in pain from an innocuous touch. The faded purple bruises that had once marred her beautiful face were a distant memory and had been replaced by an almost visible glow of contentment.

Ruby had moved into Pat's house as soon as she had been discharged from hospital to, 'get herself back on her feet,' as Pat had put it, but she was showing no signs of wanting to move on; not that Pat was in any rush for her to leave either. Truth be told, Pat was loving having someone to share her home and fill the emptiness that her beloved Alf had left behind, and she absolutely doted on Reuben who was a now a happy, cheeky little toddler. He could do no wrong in Pat's eyes, although she was currently polishing her coffee table more than she ever had!

Ruby had managed to find herself a little part time job which had gone a long way to helping her re-build her confidence, not to mention making her some of her own friends for the first time in her life. Pat was always a willing babysitter and she was the Nanny-figure to Reuben that Ruby had always dreamed of. He even went back to visit Mrs Jenkins now and again, especially on darts nights; so, he had gained two Nannies for the price of one! For the first time in her life, Ruby had a family and it felt great.

Blossom and Apryl were next to bowl through the club doors. Surprisingly, they were still together and there was even talk of a wedding; although Jude hoped to God that Blossom wasn't planning on wearing the dress!

"Alright girls?" said Blossom. "How are we all?"

"Nice to be back," said Jude.

"Hey, did you hear one of the Bacardi Brothers has died?" said Blossom, referring to a pair of friends who were frequent patrons of the labour club, and affectionately named after their overwhelming addiction to the White Rum drink.

"Which one?" asked Ruby.

"Christ knows!" exclaimed Blossom. "I couldn't tell you their names, they only ever came as a pair!"

Blossom went on to recount the events of the funeral which had been well attended by a large number of the local alcoholics and had ended in an almighty punch up. Apparently, the bouquet of flowers presented by the remaining Bacardi Brother, and in pride of place on the coffin, had been created to portray a bottle of Bacardi as a tribute – Jude laughed at the irony of such a tribute when it had clearly been the cause of death! ...A bit like sending flowers in the shape of a bus for someone who had been run over by one!

Pat returned from the bar with a tray of drinks.

"Thanks Pat," said Ruby, turning to Jude as she spoke, "You ok for tomorrow?"

Ruby was obviously referring to Little Dean's release from prison. Jude couldn't deny that she had butterflies in her tummy just thinking about, but she would be mighty glad to see her boy again without a prison guard standing behind them.

Little Dean had gone to court the week after Tommy's arrest. He had been given eight months with another 12 on licence. This meant he would be released on a tag for the remainder of his sentence. Jude had seen quite a change in her boy in the months that he had been locked away. In some ways, although she felt guilty for thinking it, she was glad he had been given time.

Being locked up had meant that he'd had a chance to miss all of the things he had taken for granted; his freedom, his family and now his baby daughter – Angelique, or Angel for short. He had entered into a drug rehab programme and had even used the time in prison to take a couple of courses in English and Maths, as well as some basic mechanic skills. Little Dean had always loved cars and bikes and Jude hoped that his training might eventually lead to him getting a job.

Chelsea had been an absolute diamond and had stuck by Little Dean, regularly going to visit him, and taking baby Angel with her. Jude couldn't have fallen more in love with the baby and she worshipped every soft, blonde curl on her head. Jude only hoped that Little Dean truly realised just how bloody fortunate he was. He'd had a lucky escape in more ways than one.

Jude was living in a tiny flat above the bakery in town where she now worked. She had genuinely tried to remain on amicable terms with her errant husband during their divorce, but she had long since given up. Dean Senior had continued to be the feckless and selfish waste of space that she now realised he had always been. He had contested the divorce at every opportunity, choosing to be as bloody difficult as possible. Jude was under no illusions that this was born out of a sense of regret for their broken marriage, nor for the fact that he wanted her to stay; she knew without a doubt that this had simply been his way of exercising what little control he still could – he was basically being a bit of a dick. No change there then! It wasn't like they had a large estate to fight over. In fact, the only thing Jude had wanted from their marriage was the dog! He could keep the poxy Queen Anne replica chair that she absolutely hated; she was happy for him to take possession of her entire knicker drawer, such as it was, if the fancy took him. She gave a lot less than two shits – she just wanted to draw a line under the whole sorry affair.

Recently, Jude had stopped pandering to his attention seeking behaviour. She had decided to ignore him until he ran out of steam which, knowing Dean, wouldn't be long! The longest he'd stuck at anything was waiting 20 minutes for a bus ride to the bookies! Since the split, he had made no effort with his son, let alone his granddaughter, and, if she was completely honest, Jude was relieved to be rid of him. She simply didn't have the patience or the energy for his shit any longer. The last Jude had heard, Dean Senior had now shacked up with the woman from the bookies and she was bloody welcome to him!

Although Jude's flat was tiny, it was prettier than anything she had ever had in her entire adult life. Her bedroom was a soft shade of moss green, with pretty curtains and a bedspread that Jude had made herself from material that she had got in the market and which looked exactly like something from a Kath Kidston catalogue. Every piece of hand-me-down furniture had been lovingly painted and re-covered and, although it wasn't posh, Jude was unbelievably proud of her little home. There was even a little cot in the corner of her room for when her little Angel came to stay; which she did whenever Jude had a spare moment!

"Yes, all good," replied Jude, snapping out of her

thoughts and replying to Ruby's question. "I just hope he doesn't muck things up again."

"He'll be alright now," said Pat. "Anyone can see the change in that boy, just by the things he says to you."

Jude couldn't deny that she barely recognised her boy at times, and she couldn't be more grateful.

"It'll be fine," said Ruby, putting her arms round Jude's shoulders. "Seems like we've all had a second chance, eh?"

Ruby, Pat and Jude looked at each other for a few moments. It was incredible how close they had all become in a relatively short time – closer than family – and how their friendship had developed out of the most unlikely circumstances; but then, didn't they say truth was stranger than fiction?

"Now then you soppy buggers," shrieked Emma placing a tray full of shot glasses in front of them and breaking the moment completely. "Get these down ya!"

"What the fuck is that?" exclaimed Pat eyeing the array of multi-coloured shots on the tray before them.

"It's the beginning of a beautiful evening!" laughed Emma, passing round the shots. "3-2-1 Down the hatch!"

Jude and Pat both winced as they 'down-ed' the indistinguishable coloured liquids.

"Tastes like bloody floor cleaner!" shrieked Pat, although Jude thought hers had tasted much worse than floor cleaner could ever have tasted!

Chapter Thirty-Three: The Prison Gate

Jude and Chelsea stood in front of the imposing iron gates that shielded the large wooden door to the prison. Angel was dressed in her very best dress, with matching bootees and a little bonnet with a pink gingham trim. She lay in her buggy, gurgling at the toys that dangled in front of her, oblivious to the tension felt by both her Mum and her Nan.

"I don't know why I'm so nervous," said Jude, her stomach in knots.

"I think he'll be alright," said Chelsea. "I've told him, I'm taking none of his shit – one slip-up and that's it. No second chances, not with this little angel to look after." She reached into the pram and tickled her daughter lovingly.

Jude was so proud of Chelsea, even though she wasn't her own flesh and blood, and the two of them had become really close.

"You're a good girl," said Jude, kissing Chelsea on the cheek. "I'm glad I've got you…whatever happens."

"Me too," said Chelsea.

Chelsea and Jude both jumped as the huge prison door swung open. Little Dean emerged into the sunlight, looking for all the world like a hatching bird. He came towards them. He looked nervous. He pulled Chelsea into him, kissing the top of her head. When he reached into the buggy to hold his precious daughter, Jude thought her heart would burst. She didn't know what the future held in store for them, but she dared to hope that things might just be ok…

THE END

Also available from Karen Stanley
The One-Legged Lady from Balmoral Road
The Tattooed Bloke in the Flat Next Door
The Path to True Love

Printed in Great Britain
by Amazon